Charms
for
the
Easy
Life

ALSO BY KAYE GIBBONS

Ellen Foster
A Virtuous Woman
A Cure for Dreams

Charms for the Easy Life

KAYE GIBBONS

G. P. PUTNAM'S SONS
NEW YORK

This novel is a work of fiction. Any references to historical events; to real people, living or dead; or to real locales are intended only to give the fiction a sense of reality and authenticity. Other names, characters, places, and incidents either are the product of the author's imagination or are used fictitiously, and their resemblance, if any, to real-life counterparts is entirely coincidental.

Copyright © 1993 by Kaye Gibbons
All rights reserved. This book, or parts thereof,
may not be reproduced in any form without permission.
Published by G. P. Putnam's Sons,
200 Madison Avenue, New York, NY 10016.
Published simultaneously in Canada

Library of Congress Cataloging-in-Publication Data

Gibbons, Kaye, date.
Charms for the easy life / Kaye Gibbons.
p.   cm.
ISBN 0-399-13791-2
I. Title.
PS3557.I13917C48   1992   92-40690 CIP
813'.54—dc20

Designed by MaryJane DiMassi
The text of this book is set in Garamond.

Printed in the United States of America
8   9   10

This book is printed on acid-free paper.
∞

for LIZ DARHANSOFF

I wish to thank the people who have helped this novel endure the past two years: Frank Ward, Karen Bethune, Susan Nutter, Faith Sale, Anna Jardine, Liz Darhansoff, and as always, my children, Louise, Leslie, and Mary. A long-overdue thanks is owed my brother, David Batts, for taking me in, dusting me off, showing me the virtues of an honest day's work, and smiling over my report cards.

I am grateful for the support and encouragement given to me by the North Carolina State University Friends of the Library and the Mobile, Alabama, Friends of the Library. I wish to recognize Ron Simpson, Dr. David Henderson, and Dr. Robert Farnham for their expert ability to answer numerous and sometimes strange questions. WPA interviews collected during the Depression and the work of Studs Terkel, particularly *The Good War,* were primary sources of inspiration for this novel.

Stupidity in a woman is unfeminine.

Friedrich Nietzsche
Human, All Too Human, 1878

ALREADY by her twentieth birthday, my grandmother was an excellent midwife, in great demand. Her black bag bulged with mysteries in vials. This occupation led her to my grandfather, whose job was operating a rope-and-barge ferry that traveled across the Pasquotank River. A heavy cable ran from shore to shore, and he pulled the cable and thus the barge carrying people, animals, everything in the world, across the river. My grandmother was a frequent passenger, going back and forth over the river to catch babies, nurse the sick, and care for the dead as well. I hear him singing as he pulls her barge. At first it may have annoyed her, but soon it was a sound she couldn't live without. She may have made up reasons to cross the river so she could hear him and see him. Think of a man content enough with quiet nights to work a river alone. Think of a man content to bathe in a river and drink from it, too. As for what he saw when he looked at my grandmother, if she looked anything like my mother's high school graduation photograph, she was dazzling, her green eyes glancing from his to the water to the shore. Between my grandmother, her green eyes and mound of black hair, and the big-cookie moon low over the Pasquotank, it must have been all my grandfather could do to deposit her on the other side of the river. Imagine what he felt when she told him her name was Clarissa Kate but she insisted on being called Charlie Kate. She probably told him that Clarissa was a spineless name.

Now, some facts of her life I have not had to half invent by dream. She and my grandfather were married by a circuit rider in 1902 and lived in a tiny cabin on the Pasquotank, completely cut off from everybody but each other. My grandmother continued to nurse people who lived across the river, and soon Indian women in the vicinity came to prefer her root cures to their own. My mother was born here in 1904. She was delivered by an old Indian woman named Sophia Snow, thus her name, Sophia Snow Birch. My grandmother became hung in one of those long, deadly labors common to women of the last century. After thirty-six hours of work with little result, my grandmother decided she would labor standing, holding on to the bedpost for support, letting gravity do what it would. Sophia, however, persuaded her to be quilled, and so a measure of red pepper was blown up my grandmother's nose through the end of a feather freshly plucked from one of her many peacocks. My grandmother fell into a sneezing frenzy, and when she recovered enough to slap Sophia, she did. Sophia slapped her back, earning both my grandmother's respect and an extra dollar. Within the hour, my mother was born.

She told me she had a wild-animal sort of babyhood. She remembered the infant bliss of sunning on a pallet while her mother tended her herbs. Her parents kept sheep on free range in the yard, and my mother told me how she had stood by a caldron and soaked the wool down into indigo with a boat paddle twice as tall as she was. She said to me, "We were like Pilgrim settlers. Everything had to be done, and we did everything."

They left Pasquotank County in 1910. The suicide of Camelia, my grandmother's twin sister, made it impossible for her to stay there. They were so bound together that as small children, when they slept in the same crib, they awakened every morning each sucking the other's thumb. Grief for Camelia hounded my grandmother from the place where her family had lived for five generations. Within days after Camelia's hydrocephalic son died, his wildly sorrowful father wandered out and lay like one already dead across the railroad tracks, to be run over by the afternoon train. Camelia lost her mind immediately. My grandmother implored her sister to come stay with her, but she would not. She stayed alone in her house and handled baby clothes and wrung her hands in the clothes of her husband and baby until these clothes and she herself were shredded and unrecognizable. My grandmother would go each day and change Camelia's soiled dresses and linens while she walked all through the house naked, moaning, "Oh, my big-headed baby! Oh, the man I adored!"

Just when my grandmother was wondering how much worse things would become, Camelia developed a fixation on Teddy Roosevelt, writing love letters to the White House which were opened at the local post office and made available to anyone who wanted a good snicker. The Roosevelt fixation continued a long time, too long, as told by the fact that when Camelia's body was found, with great razor gashes at her neck, wrists, and elbows, there was a note from her idea of Mr. Roosevelt on her kitchen table. It said:

> Dere Camelia,
>   go an git yor belovet husbendzs razer and take it to bed wit yu.
>   it wuz a mistak the babi bean born. go be wit him and yor belovet in paridiz.
>
> Luv Sinserle,
Theodor

Among her other personal effects, my grandmother found more than a hundred notes Camelia had written to herself from Mr. Roosevelt.

My grandfather did not want to leave Pasquotank County, but the government's decision to scrap the ferry for a modern steel bridge satisfied my grandmother's urgent need to leave. She was so relieved that her sighs all but created wind. The only decision they needed to make was where to go. They chose Wake County because my grandfather was convinced that this was a place overflowing with gorgeous opportunities even for an illiterate barge operator.

He had never been to Wake County himself, but he had ferried a great many of what he took to be highly respectable gentlemen from there. I bet they were not. I bet he simply had no basis for comparison, and that these men were just farmers in clean clothes. Southern gentlemen would not have had a call to visit the far side of the Pasquotank. There was nobody there, in short, to give them any money.

On the way to Wake County, something happened. They stopped and cut a man down from a lynching. This poor man was alive but barely, and after my grandmother rubbed voice back into his throat with her bare hands, he sat up and regarded the botched execution with great contempt. He rode with my grandparents the rest of the way to Wake County, sitting beside my mother in the buggy, telling her hoarsely again and again, "They will come and look at that tree and have to wonder. I bet they'll bet Jesus took me down. They won't come looking for me now, not with the power of God in me." He thanked my grandparents with a railroad watch, a tin of excellent snuff, and an easy-life charm he pulled off a greasy thin chain around his ankle. (The charm, he said, was the hind foot of a white graveyard rabbit caught at midnight, under the full moon, by a cross-eyed Negro woman who had been married seven times.) He then walked around this part of the state for the rest of his life with a thick scar around his throat, singing my grandmother's praises. He talked his salvation into legend.

My mother's family didn't arrive poor. My grandmother's savings as well as the stock she inherited from a wealthy landowner whom she had once treated for syphilis made her a woman of surprisingly comfortable means. But because she lacked the social position commensurate with her robust financial portfolio, she couldn't live in the surroundings she deserved. Instead, she purchased the best house in the Beale Street area, the worst part of town. My mother always approved of this, saying, "If we had moved where my mother could've very easily afforded, nobody would've played with me, Daddy would've had nobody to drink with, and she would've had to suffer notes on the door telling her she couldn't plant that much bloodroot and sassafras in the front yard."

My grandmother soon created suspicion within the neighborhood anyway. She woke up one morning to find a petition nailed to her front door. It read: "The redio cawsd it so git rit ov it." Ten neighbors actually signed the petition, or rather, six signed and four X'd. The week before, she had acquired a radio, which ran off a low wire strung across the backyard, and that weekend a tornado touched down and leveled a row of shotgun houses, killing dairy cows, chickens, and (sad to say) a small boy. It reduced many people with next to nothing to nothing. And then somebody must have asked the question: What spoilt the sky? I imagine somebody recalling the strange wire stretched across the new family's yard, and thus the petition. My grandmother solved this matter by inviting people into the house one evening to listen to an experimental broadcast of news, religious music, and inspirational poetry on her radio, and while they were there she removed warts, cut out bunions, mixed laxatives, and applied a salt-and-soda swab to a hideous case of pyorrhea. My grandfather delighted the men in the crowd with samples of Pasquotank moonshine and empty promises that there was plenty more where that came from. By ten o'clock my grandmother was having to push a host of new, loyal patients out the door, along with their inebriated husbands and my mother's sleepy new playmates.

My grandfather scrounged around for work. Finally he took a job he loathed, saying it was thoroughly beneath his dignity. The longer he worked this contemptible job, the more dignity he imagined he had lost. He was, for want of a better term, a gofer for a blacksmith. He wasn't allowed to shoe the horses, just tote the ashes. As he became more and more frustrated with his life, he became, understandably, more and more unbearable. My grandmother secretly withdrew her affection and offered more of herself to caring for my mother and her patients and achieving local fame for hygienic improvements in not only her home but others'. Although improvements such as sidewalks and modern plumbing were common in other parts of town, the mill district had been neglected because, as my grandmother put it, "the people there didn't count as people." She shamed the owner of the textile mill into installing wide boardwalks beside two particularly soupy streets by asking him point-blank how he slept at night knowing children were wading to school through mud and the gore from the meat-packing house up the hill. As for bringing the area onto the city sewage lines, she succeeded by reminding the city council of a fact it was (shocking to say) not aware of: that the residents of this tiny district were all white, not a colored person among them. Years later she told me, "It shouldn't have made any difference to them. That it mattered one iota was criminal." After the sewer lines were installed, the director of the public works department wrote her a note of commendation in which he actually said that if he had realized the Beale Street area was all white, he would've installed the lines long before.

Whenever someone had a toilet put in, a message would be sent for my grandmother to go and give a lesson. For many people, a toilet remained a long time as something they stared at. My grandmother was to be remembered for many achievements, from campaigning for in-school vaccinations to raising money to buy prosthetics for veterans of the World War, but in the Beale Street area of Raleigh she lives in the memory of an old few as the first woman anybody knew with the courage not only to possess a toilet but to use it.

She developed a fantastic trade, with sick people coming forth like the loaves and the fishes, putting one real doctor in such danger of losing patients that he sent her a nice note and a ten-dollar bill. This only encouraged her. She put the word out that she knew how to fix teeth, even though she did not. What she knew was that everybody in 1910 needed this done, and once they were at the house, she inquired after their other ailments and cured what she knew how to cure, and astounded people into forgetting about their teeth. When she finally branched out into dentistry, she did so because, as she said, it was easy money. Her instruments were needle-nose pliers and a wrench, both ordered from

Sears, Roebuck, her anesthesia was chloroform ordered from a veterinary supply firm, and her technique came straight from *Dr. John C. Gunn's Domestic Medicine: The Poor Man's Friend in the House of Affliction, Pain and Sickness.* What is most fascinating with regard to her dentistry is that she would put women patients under, but work on the men as is. She believed that although women, as a rule, could stand more pain and take more punishment than men, they should not have to and would not ever suffer under her care. She told me that her women patients loved chloroform, the feeling of falling backward and forgetting for a while about diapers and laundry and supper. The degree to which a woman looked tired in the face dictated the amount of chloroform she received, and sometimes when my grandmother recognized that a woman was too taxed by her life, she did her the favor of knocking her out to the point that she could neither lift her head nor say her name the rest of the day. She said, "Some of these women, if they didn't have me work on their mouths, they'd never have gotten off their feet."

My mother, during this time, was happy as pie, going to elementary school, coming home and wrapping bandages, pressing pills, helping with supper, doing her homework by the fire. She first witnessed an operation performed by her mother in 1911, when she was seven. So much blood was involved that they could never fully scrub it out of the cracks in the kitchen linoleum. A man from the sawmill in back of their house suffered a horrible accident, and as the company doctor was not to be found, the man was rushed to my grandmother's kitchen table. She sewed him up with the only thread she had, red cotton, and nursed him back to health. He slept in my mother's bed and ate liver three times a day for a week. My mother slept on a warm pallet by the woodstove, waking up those mornings with the odor of liver burning her nose. The man taught my mother how to play whist and also how to make the spirits rap under the card table. For payment, my grandmother requested that the sawmill hire the best carpenter in town to build a lovely addition onto her home. Otherwise, she said, the world would know about the loose blades, loose belts, and unoiled machinery that she'd heard about as the victim ate his dinner.

As time passed, my grandparents had less and less to say to each other. There was no fighting, since they couldn't find anything between them they cared enough to fight about. My grandfather would come home from a day of toting ashes at the livery stable, eat, and then sit and watch his wife grind herbs or read used medical textbooks. He would fall asleep watching her, and eventually she stopped bothering to wake him to go lie down in his comfortable bed. She would let him sleep upright in a chair all night and would walk out of the room when he complained of a stiff neck in the morning. My mother told me, "He would sit there and sigh and shake his head, watching her become better and better at what she loved. He admired her, I think, but all the same, he couldn't bear it."

After just two years in Wake County, they were at the point of completely wordless meals, wordless evenings, wordless Sundays. My grandfather was destined to leave this sort of situation, so he left. He left the way sad men leave: he did not come home from work. Maybe he missed a river, because this is where he went—not to the Pasquotank, as there was nothing there for him, but west to the Ohio. I imagine he went there without stopping. I think of him not eating or sleeping until he got there. (That sort of hurling oneself at a desire is a family trait, and has made convicts, scholars, lovers, and dope fiends out of us from way back.) He reportedly had a grand time on the Ohio without his wife. Travelers carted home tales of my grandfather's loving Ohio Valley women galore.

How did my grandmother react when her husband let his supper get so cold? She let his dishes sit at his place overnight, and then the next morning she threw them in the sink and broke them every one, yelling, "To hell with him!" She left his clothes in the closet, which was a sign to my mother, even so young. My grandmother had no friends or acquaintances other than her patients, so there were no rounds of explaining to be made. Nobody would be watching her to see how she managed. Nobody would note the breadth of her pride. Well, nobody except my mother, who watched and learned. This is what she learned: A man will leave you.

Did my mother miss him? She told me that at the time she did not. I asked how a child could not miss her father. She said, "I was busy. I was highly involved in the life of my second grade." What she meant is that she had learned to read. She was the sort of curious child, I would think, who is transformed by school. These children become adults too soon, but seemingly happy ones, and content. But then, later in her life, when she needed a memory of tenderness to reconcile what she lacked with my father, she must have relived the evening her father's dinner sat waiting, and that next morning, and the next night, and on and on and on.

My mother spent much of her childhood riding back and forth to funerals in Pasquotank County. Although the suicide of my grandmother's sister had driven her away from home, she was called back several times to wash the bodies of other relatives who had done the same thing. In 1917 she buried two cousins who became despondent after they read their father's name on a wartime casualty list at the train station. The ground opened up and swallowed them, standing together reading the wall. That evening at supper somebody broke a pitcher, and these girls secreted the glass into their bosoms and went down to the root cellar and used the fragments. Double blood flowed everywhere, soaking the bottoms of the wooden baskets that held all the family's winter food. A few days after my grandmother returned home, her aunt hired a gypsy to conduct a silly and desperate midnight séance, and after he was told the story of all the blood in the basement, he said that potatoes had eyes and had not only seen but soaked up the sight of the two girls in the back corner. He volunteered to relieve the family of this evil food, promising to burn the bushels in a fire on sacred ground somewhere, together with a lock of hair of

John the Baptist or some other saint. As gypsies were inclined to do, he rode away with the family's winter food and
was never seen again. When my grandmother was asked to
send money so they could eat that winter, she would not.
She let them grieve hungry.

Her family did not speak to her until they needed her again,
a year later, for another burial. She went, taking my fourteen-
year-old mother with her to sit at the wake and occupy her
mind writing morbid poetry in her diary. The uncle my
grandmother washed and laid out had spent the last five years
of his life so bent down and twisted back on himself with
arthritis that parts of his body that had ceased to get light and
air had molded. He hated his life, and told everyone he knew
how anxious he was to end it. After supper one evening he
wandered off into the woods, where he was found the next
morning, stretched out as if sleeping, with a basket half full of
the kinds of things he had eaten: death-cap mushrooms, yew
bark, juniper berries, a sliver of root from the mayapple, and
much, much more. My grandmother's family had, by this
time, become so embarrassed over their remarkable suicide
rate that they denied the old man had died of anything other
than natural causes. For all time, they would say, "He didn't
kill himself. He died of arthritis."

This dismissal of the truth angered my grandmother so
much that she vowed not to speak to her family again, no
matter who was dying or dead. She would let them rot in
Pasquotank County. My mother remembered her standing
on her aunt's porch and screaming, "You can all jump in the
goddamn river and drown and see if I come and lay you

out!" My mother remembered how she stood there in the middle of the yard, how she could see her mother's back and her hands on her hips, and how, behind the house, the Pasquotank River roared. She told me that the first thing she figured out about life was why none of these relatives jumped in that river, convenient as it was. She said, "I knew I was smart when I checked my answer with my mother, and she said I was right. She bought me a bag of hard candy as a reward for reasoning out a bit of the universe."

This is why, as my mother imagined, six members of my grandmother's family used variously violent and painful means to kill themselves, without a thought of jumping in the river that ran by their doors: They threatened to kill themselves in the river all the time. They used the threat in arguments with each other. They said the words without thinking, which was something my mother had already noticed that every adult in the world, except for her mother, did. *If you don't stop it with that other woman, I'm going to jump in the river. If you don't stop chewing with your mouth open, I'm going to jump in the river.* But they didn't go in the river, because the river was life to them, life all surging and all crashing into white foam on river rocks they had known their whole lives, and the thought of throwing themselves into a familiar current and banging choked and goggle-eyed against rocks they had stood on and courted on and fished and dreamed on, and sat in the sun and dared to open their blouses and nurse their babies on, this was not something they could do. They would walk fifty miles and jump in some other person's river, but not their own.

FOR MY MOTHER to have been so smart so young, her powers of reason failed her in 1922, when she married a cad. To assuage a great deal of the blame I at times placed on her for not having supplied me with a more intelligent, thoughtful, and attentive father, I told myself that the marriage was the natural and inevitable consequence of her father's disappearance.

When he married my mother, my father wore a pair of yellow shoes he acquired from a pickpocket being held in custody in the magistrate's office where their vows were hurriedly spoken. He thought this was funny, and had my mother been of the same mind, maybe it would've been. Instead, she was horrified, and if she had not been so stubbornly committed to the marriage, she would've left him at the altar, such as it was. The chief scent at her wedding was raw onion, the odor carried by the deputy sheriff who served as witness and goaded my father into trying on the yellow shoes. "They were all having a jolly time," she told me. "I felt like I wasn't there."

The person who really was not there was my grandmother, who saw through all things and knew that my mother was marrying this man because he was witty, clever, and good-looking and because he didn't turn back the affection that my mother heaped on him. He was just what a young woman who was lonesome for a father craved. His ego was as vast as her passion, which had threatened her scholarship and caused the headmistress of Miss Nash's School for Young Ladies to remark on several occasions that my mother's boundless energy, her refusal to hide her ankles, and her insistence on reciting Oscar Wilde at assembly was almost more than she could bear. She asked my grandmother to check her daughter's tendencies toward freethinking, as this would cause her a life of general unease and calamity. My grandmother did nothing of the sort. She encouraged my mother in all endeavors except when it came to her choice of suitors.

My mother was drawn to wickedly handsome boys who could not marry her because of constraints placed on them by their social class and their mothers, boys who lacked the will to override either in favor of my mother, no matter how refreshing and spirited they considered her to be. She showed no interest at all in the young man my grandmother handpicked for her, and he showed none in her, the chief reason being that he was seven years her senior. Even with such an obstacle, my grandmother's inability to bring the two together must have made her doubt the magnetic capabilities of her enormous will. He was a remarkable person, and for days after I heard about him, I was mad at my mother for not having allowed me the emotional, intellectual, and financial rewards of being his daughter. His name was Charles Nutter, and he was reared on the far side of the Pasquotank. When my grandmother returned there periodically to care for the boy's pathetically lunatic and tubercular mother, who wouldn't let any other person treat her, she noticed what she always referred to as his light and wit, and she made sure he had money to buy schoolbooks and studying materials. It was during this time that my grandmother began to see him as the perfect son-in-law. On weekend trips she would collect my mother from Miss Nash's School and talk of this brilliant young man all the way to Pasquotank County. He always seemed more concerned with books my grandmother brought him than he seemed with her little daughter, but I know my grandmother believed this would change in time, and so for three years she contented herself with exposing these two young people to each other.

Charles Nutter studied incessantly and accumulated a treasury of knowledge, much in the manner of a young Lincoln, with whom he was later to be compared. By his tenth year in school the superintendent was the only person in Pasquotank County who was not too intimidated to teach him. While his backwater peers were ciphering naughts and double-naughts on chipped slates, their grubby hands no doubt rubbing out errors at every turn, Charles was reading Horace and Virgil under plantation fans in the county office building, the portly superintendent marking his rhythms with a metronome. (Think of what a sleepy-making time that must have been!) Charles worked nights and summers collecting pond specimens for Carolina Biological Supply, a job my grandmother got for him by writing to the company and announcing when he could start. On many Saturday afternoons my grandmother sat on the riverbank and watched him and my mother wading about in the shallow waters, my mother with her skirt tied into her belt, helping him skim for tadpoles and insect larvae. I imagine my grandmother wondering when he would notice my mother's trim ankles, pretty calves and knees, when he would look at her and realize she might grow up quite nicely. I imagine him too preoccupied with his specimens and his future to notice.

He graduated from high school in 1914 with a superb record and was begged to attend several colleges, although as my grandmother put it, none of them begged to pay his way. And there was more begging, that of his mother, who threatened to die if he left her. My grandmother interceded, as she often did in needy lives, first by packing the mother off for a rest cure in Asheville and then by sending the boy's high school records to the Office of Undergraduate Admissions at the University of North Carolina at Chapel Hill, along with a deposit for his first semester of enrollment. She believed he was a better investment than Great Atlantic & Pacific Tea, so she sold enough of this company's stock to send him to both undergraduate and medical school at Chapel Hill.

So Charles was educated thanks to my grandmother. He

completed the undergraduate program in just two years, and by his second year of medical school, her investment began paying off. I do not mean paying off in the sense that he made her proud, made his community proud, or dutifully repaid his loan at a trudging-along rate of a quarter a week. Nothing of that nature. Instead, something spectacular, at least for the time and place and for one so young. In 1918 he patented the design for a much-needed and humane prosthetic device for returning World War I soldiers, a well-fitting vulcanized rubber and metal contraption that made the young men feel less like Captain Hook. He was commended not only by President Wilson but by the French and British governments as well. He sold the patent to a New York firm, and while it was never clear exactly how much money he made, it was enough to build a new one-room Pasquotank Normal School and hire a teacher whose literacy was not in constant doubt.

My grandmother believed that with medical school behind Charles Nutter and puberty behind my mother, things could finally start to happen between the two. But despite her urging, neither of them could be talked into carrying the relationship forward. They enjoyed each other's company, but as my mother later told me, "We were not what we were looking for. I needed a boy and he needed a woman. Both of us wanted her to stop playing Cupid."

Then along came my father, who turned my mother's head completely around in her collar. His family had recently made so much money so quickly in land speculation that they had torn their old house down to the foundation and built a replica of their plantation ideal in its place. Being members of the emerging class of newly rich, they didn't know any better than to accept happily the bold daughter of an even bolder self-proclaimed doctor. She was beautiful and quick, and they loved her like a daughter right away. My father courted her against my grandmother's wishes for a year. He proposed to her the day she was awarded her diploma from Miss Nash's School. His family gave her fifty acres of land outright as a wedding gift, more than any of their children owned, and then during a Sunday supper they asked her to sketch her dream house on a linen napkin. It was built immediately, and then furnished with the best of everything that could be shipped from New Orleans, Savannah, New York, and Boston. This was completed weeks before the wedding. My mother would go sit in the new house that was so full of all her new things and think of her future, and then she'd go back to her mother's house and go to sleep hearing her mother rap on her bedroom door, saying things like, "Time is ticking, but it's not too late to change your mind."

She would not change her mind. The week before my parents were married, my father graduated from the North Carolina Agricultural Institute and was made the Wake County extension agent, a position he held until his death. (Let it be known that he was given the job because of his wealthy father's influence and stayed there as long as he did because of his pretty secretary's desires.) My mother used his responsible position to defend him, but this was batted back by my grandmother, who sat her down and explained that marrying a man who didn't need to work would make her miserable within six months. She said he would wear the new off my mother and then grow bored, the same way an overly bright child becomes bored in a classroom and makes trouble to excite his day and titillate his spirit. He would range around seeking his pleasures, looking right through my mother as if she were invisible. My grandmother said, "All these things will happen. I'll hide and watch them."

My mother refused to acknowledge her fear that any of the predictions would come true, although I can see her as the petulant childlike beauty she could be, shifting about in her seat, her lips poked out, arms crossed, breathing in quick little pants as the horror of her mistake was revealed to her. She would've tried to pass her squirming off as exasperation with her mother's meddling, but her anxiety had nothing to do with her mother. She was too bright not to have known everything her mother said was true, but she would've stuck her hands in a fan or swallowed lye before admitting this. My grandmother's final words were, "Marry him, and I will not set foot in your house until you beg me." She was fully aware that she had not raised the kind of child who would beg for anything, not water in the desert, not bread in a famine, and my mother was aware that her mother's famous will would keep her out of a house that was only two miles from her own, even on holidays, even on the occasion of my birth in 1924.

On the other hand, my mother and I *were* allowed to go to my grandmother's house, and so we visited there every weekend, and left my father early Christmas mornings, and every Easter and New Year's Day. But we never spoke of him in her presence. We never mentioned our house, new furniture, new wallpaper or carpeting, and there was never any discussion of when or whether the curse of absence would be lifted. It was as if we walked from nowhere and appeared at my grandmother's door, but this did not in any way diminish the grand time we had there. We made beignets and drank chickory and played nurse when patients appeared at my grandmother's door. My mother and grandmother would sit at the kitchen table and discuss investments, studying a company prospectus spread out in front of them the way other women would've pointed out new fashions in a department store advertisement. When they reached a decision, we would all ride to town and meet with my grandmother's broker at Wheat First Securities, who praised her as an intrepid investor in spite of the fact that she would never buy anything on margin.

Also on those weekends and holidays at my grandmother's, I listened to many discussions of what my mother was going to do with her life besides read, listen to the radio, volunteer at the Red Cross office, and manage a tidy and efficient household, which amounted to sitting at the breakfast table with Maveen, our combination housekeeper, cook, laundress, and gardener, and listing the daily chores. To most middle-class Southern women of the day, this was more than enough, but to my grandmother it amounted to no more than passing time, waiting for the brittle bones and palsy of old age. The only thing my mother did that my grandmother approved of, besides reading, was teaching me beyond my daily school lessons. On Saturdays my grandmother would ask right away what I had learned that week, and if I said my fourth-grade class was reading "Rip Van Winkle," she would squint and push her face forward to ask my mother if she had gotten "The Legend of Sleepy Hollow" from the library yet. It gave my mother a world's worth of satisfaction to answer, "Yes, and we're already halfway through it." My grandmother had spent her childhood receiving parcels of books from the Olivia Raney Library in Raleigh. She told me once, with great assurance, "I have read two books a week for thirty years. I am satisfied that I know everything."

Many times my mother and I rode with my grandmother to nurse her family in Pasquotank County. I spent most of my time there playing with cousins, but in 1928 my mother and grandmother took me along on a mission that my mother later characterized as bizarre. I was four years old, and thus the memory cannot be presented as my own. My mother and grandmother told me the story. The three of us drove to Pasquotank County to pick up my grandmother's oldest sister, and then took her on to Richmond, where her son had just shot himself after having spent two miserable years grieving over the death of Rudolph Valentino. This was the last in the family's cluster of suicides. We were taking my great-aunt to collect her son's belongings from a gentlemen's boardinghouse and make arrangements for his body to be brought back to North Carolina. She sat by my grandmother in the front seat, kneading her hands, screaming, "How did it come to this?" She would lean forward every now and then and pound her fists on the dashboard, and my grandmother would snap, "This is a new automobile! Don't ruin it!" My great-aunt's son had escaped Pasquotank and gone to Richmond when he was thirteen, and by twenty he was working as a doorman at a swank hotel. The few sightings of him that made their way back home had him prancing up and down in front of the hotel between patrons, checking his bearing and demeanor in the big brass doors, hissing at people who stopped to stare at him. My grandmother had to trick his mother into leaving the room while she bagged the sad scrapings of a depraved and lonely life and flushed them down the toilet. "Drugs and pills of every nature," she told me. When his mother came in and opened a dresser drawer that my grandmother had somehow skipped, she said, "Oh, Charlie Kate. He had a girlfriend. Look at all her things here. I always knew what people said about him wasn't so." Think of this! Think of a mother so desperate for a normal son that in 1928 she was not only ready but eager to excuse his dalliance outside the bounds of marriage. My grandmother had read journal articles pertaining to "aberrant behavior," and while his mother sat on his bed and successfully wished herself into seeing her son row some pretty girl across a moonlit lake, my grandmother stuffed the dreamland girlfriend's things into a paper sack and marveled that a man could cram his feet into shoes so high and narrow.

On Saturdays when no patients showed up, when no calls came in, when the three of us didn't drive to Pasquotank, my mother and grandmother would write and send out birthday cards to children in Wake County. Once a week, my grandmother called the office where birth certificates were registered, and thus her wooden file box was always up-to-date. Names of children she had delivered were denoted with stars, and she would tape a nickel inside their cards, and children who were turning thirteen received another gift, instruction in sexual hygiene that a legislative committee had praised as the true reason for Wake County's modest rate of illegitimacy.

For the boys, she ordered ready-made pamphlets from a distributor, and then wrote at the top of the cover page: "On the occasion of your thirteenth birthday. Read and hide from Mama, Papa, Sister, and Brother." Inside, she would correct the hygienic instruction however she saw fit, as with the scalding condemnation of what was called "self-love." She would type out her own warning and paste it over the original. Hers read: "Better to handle yourself than some girl. You do not know where she's been. You will not become a blind lunatic nor a rabid dog-boy. In fact, it may improve your attitude and render you less likely to get in scrapes at recess. You may be a more pleasant fellow all around for following your instincts in the PRIVACY of your room." All but one of the county's seventh-grade teachers were thoughtful and alert enough to ask boys who were poor readers to bring their pamphlets to school, and they would keep the boys inside during recess and read my grandmother's instruction aloud.

There existed no similar tracts for young girls, but my grandmother broadcast information anyway. On the girls' birthday cards she would write the time and date she would arrive in person and tell them, literally, what was what. She took each of them a package marked "Moon-Time Things," and inside were little muslin sacks marked "False Unicorn for Cramps"; "Evening Primrose Oil for Moodiness"; "Goldenseal for Itching"; "Horehound for Bloating." She explained girls' bodies to them, corrected ruinous impressions created by the Baptists, and always ended her discussions with the same message I was to hear more times than a few: "Kiss all you want to. Kissing's fine, nothing more than uptown shopping on downtown business. But if you suffer him to put that ugly thing in you before you're married, do not come to me to ask how to undo what you have so stupidly done."

For THREE DAYS in 1936, when I was twelve, I sprawled my body on our divan much in the manner of Oscar Wilde, who was still a favorite of my mother's, although his influence was considered no less corruptive than it had been during her years at Miss Nash's School. I lay there refusing to budge until my father allowed me to attend the wake of my closest friend. Her name was Ida O'Shea, and she could, of all things, knit and crochet like a woman. She had been sick with a rampaging flu and had not been able to play with me all week. One Friday morning her alternately abusive and negligent mother had left her asleep at home with a spiking fever to go around and deliver the fine laundry she did weekly for town ladies, and when she returned she saw that the child had choked on her own vomit.

My parents argued about my demand continuously. Although my father's only justification was, "It will not be good for her," he said it with such vehemence that I started to wonder what he might know that my mother and I didn't. This lasted only until my mother screamed that his chief problem in life was his inability to look anything in the face, and this trait would not be passed along to me. Then they fought over what exactly he couldn't face, the answer being his unfaithfulness, the way he lived his life fidgeting to get out of the house and meet some woman somewhere. I knew the fight wasn't so much over my demand to attend the wake as it was an opportunity for them to fight over which one loved the other less. My mother finally won by reminding him that she had let him do as he pleased for years, that she had borne the strain of a life without his love and respect, that she was appalled that he could pronounce on my emotional well-being when he couldn't keep up with my birthday. He left with the promise that he'd be back when he pleased, and this meant two or three days. It always had. I know he spent at least part of his time complaining of our intransigence to his girlfriend, who no doubt impressed him with her ability to listen, a trait a wayward husband looks for in a woman. Even if the woman was a lonelyheart who would've listened to anything for any amount of time, I'm sure he was able to convince both himself and her that my mother was a shrew. People like him thrive on fantasy in the manner of children and criminals.

Once he was gone, my mother told me to bathe, and then dress in black. I remember feeling as if I had at last been given permission to go to the circus. If anything of the morbidity of what I was about to do passed through my mind, it was only that I was going to Ida's house to play dead with her. My mother said that while I was dressing she would telephone my grandmother to see if she wanted to go. I became even more excited, knowing that my grandmother attended every wake within a twenty-mile radius of her house, having laid out most of the bodies herself. She called them big coffee-drinks. Grieving families were touched by her presence, never blaming her for deaths of loved ones; they understood that if their relatives could have been healed, she would have healed them.

It was dusk when we got to my grandmother's. She was waiting by the road, wearing the same mourning garb her mother had worn from the time of Sherman's march until she died, when it had to be taken off so she could be buried in her wedding dress, according to her wishes. And yes, it did look worse for wear, but if someone had asked my grandmother whom she most resembled standing on the side of the road rearranging this black cobwebby dress around her body, she would've responded: Queen Victoria.

Before the Depression, country deaths were the odor of camphor and chrysanthemums, yet in the worst of these times deaths were just the odor of camphor, flowers being too great an expense for mourners to bear. I could smell the camphor before we were in the door, and I sank down onto the bottom step of the child's house. Terror and nausea struck together and held me down, for how long I cannot say. I remember holding my knees up to my chest, feeling the new rises in my black dress, and saying to my mother and grandmother through my tears, "Ida was so proud of her brassiere." I looked up at my grandmother, and for the first time in my life this woman who doled out compassion in thimblefuls took my hands and pulled me up into her chest and said, "You're my little bird. If we don't go in, you'll always wonder."

I walked through the house sandwiched so tightly between my mother and grandmother that had I lifted my feet off the floor I would've been carried along. I clung to my grandmother's dress so hard that later in the evening she asked my mother to repair the rip underneath her sleeve. She didn't sew, or wouldn't. We went directly to the coffee urn and then took our seats. My grandmother poured swallows of coffee into her saucer for me. I wasn't the only child there. Three children from the community had been scrubbed raw and starched in gum arabic and were sitting bolt upright on the sofa. As I sat and stared at the brown spots on my grandmother's hand, one of the children began to cough. She had what we called smothering sickness, and there with the room so stifling-thick with oil smoke and camphor, she struggled to breathe. Her mother snapped from across the room, "For Jesus' sake, take a deep breath!" My grandmother told me to sit and be still, and she went over to the child and rubbed her back and told her how to breathe on slow counts of "one-Mississippi, two-Mississippi." The child's mother said, "Thank you, Charlie Kate. I hope I don't owe you anything." My grandmother didn't react to this at all. She came back and sat beside me and said, "When you're ready to go over by Ida, tell me. Otherwise, we'll drink all their coffee and go home."

If I craned my neck, I could see the coffin well enough from where I sat. I forced myself to do this once. Ida had always been such a slip of a thing, with pale gray eyes and a tiny uplifted nose, both of which she despised and yearned to trade for what my mother had always termed my aggressive features. Because of the way she was propped, I could see only the ruffles on her favorite dress, and her beautiful nose. She seemed to be sniffing the air above her, which curdled with the camphor and the corned beef and cabbage her mother boiled perpetually. I couldn't see this from where I sat, but I assumed that her leftover medicine was beside her, brown bottles of tonic my grandmother had prescribed for dehydration. Camphor rags soaked in two tin buckets on the floor at either end of the coffin, and at one point her wailing mother hobbled up and freshened the rags in full view of us all. I had seen this same mother beat Ida and her brother with an old corset stay. I remember pulling my legs up into my seat and nudging my head up underneath my grandmother's arm like a cat. She smelled of Mavis powder and mothballs. My mother was on the other side of me with one hand gripping my thigh. She smelled of her lavender bath. I asked my grandmother if I could go home with her. She nodded that I could. My mother whispered, "Can I go, too?" She nodded again.

That night I fell asleep in my grandmother's feather bed to dream not at all. The next morning I found a valerian root underneath my pillow and was brought clover tea to drink. I convalesced at her house for four days, wearing her ancient nightgown and her ancient pantaloons, watching my mother read, looking up at my grandmother every now and then, asking without asking how she could ever return to her sad house, asking if there might be some measure of virtue in retreat. I wonder whether my grandmother had been asking herself that since she left Pasquotank County and Camelia's memory and all the Roosevelt letters she buried by her grave. I was strong enough to go home, but that in no way meant I wanted to. My grief had been plain and unpoetic, and the hole in my heart would've grown wide enough and deep enough to consume me had my mother and grandmother not kept me with them, and still. My grandmother put me to sleep those afternoons and evenings by reading to me from *The New England Journal of Medicine, The Old Farmer's Almanac,* and *The Atlanta Constitution.* I became fascinated with her mind, enamored of her muscular soul.

My father came home late on the evening my mother and I returned home. He made no excuses, offered no apologies. He passed the table where my mother and I sat playing Chinese checkers, and went to bed. My mother slept with me. The next day was Saturday, Maveen's day off, a day I had always associated with eating a roast beef platter at the Sir Walter Hotel, but that day my mother and I ate at home because she couldn't work the swelling out of her face. She had cried so long and so hard that her face was puffed into one large, pink welt. This is what had happened to her: She had gone into the bedroom early in the morning and picked my father's clothes up off the floor. Cleaning out his pockets, she found his wedding band. She shook him awake and asked him why it was there and not on his finger. He mumbled, "It hurts her feelings." Then he rolled over and went back to sleep. He slept until noon.

In the meantime, we went to my grandmother's. She was sitting at her white metal table pressing pills. My mother told her the story, making large motions with her arms. When she finished, she said, "I want you to do something about him, not kill him, but make him sick. I've had enough."

My grandmother said she could not do it. "I can make them well," she said, "but I will not make them sick."

My mother tried to change her mind, but it didn't work. My grandmother finally cut her off by saying, "Don't worry yourself. I've seen him out and about places. He's due for a stroke of paralysis or something nastier. His facial capillaries are exploding daily, even the ones on his ears, a true sign of something ugly to come. But even if that weren't the case, I wouldn't make him sick. You know I never do that."

She had a certain integrity in that regard. She refused to cross over the line from natural medicine into black magic, although in many cases, if she had not combined useless folk remedies with treatments she judged to be therapeutic, her uneducated and overly superstitious patients would not have trusted her. But still, she had to remind people of what she would and would not do for them. I had heard her tell patients many times, "I do not perform voodoo. I do not even dabble." Once I watched her throw a young man out of her house because he would not accept her refusal to conjure his wife. He wanted to hire my grandmother at an inflated rate to toss a bag of cemetery dirt into his yard at midnight. His wife had been unfaithful, and this particular hex, he believed, would keep the woman in a constant state of disappointment. My grandmother said, "If she's living with you, she's that way already. Get out of here and never come back." She wouldn't deal in the psyche, unless a broken heart, for example, had played on the nerves and thrown a body off kilter. This was the case the day I watched her wrap a piece of valerian root in bleached muslin for a young woman who had ground all the enamel off her back teeth. She had been thrown over for, I was sure, a prettier and smarter girl. She wasn't so smart and pretty. She asked my grandmother what she should do if sleeping with the valerian root underneath her pillow for the prescribed seven nights did not work. My grandmother looked up from the seven-knotted string she was tying around the muslin and said: "Get over him."

My father was dead in two months. My first monthly started the week he died. This is what may have happened to him: One evening my mother called God to the house, and He came. People look for God their entire lives, but all my mother had to do was whisper, "I need you. Hurry." He no doubt knocked Himself out getting to her, as she was such a trophy among his creations. My mother was sitting up in bed, working on her cuticles. He asked her what He could do for her, what she most desired. She looked over at my father sleeping and breathing in his gurgling, vulgar way, and He knew. He must have told my mother to go to sleep. He promised her a dream, something lush she would enjoy.

She wouldn't notice the sudden quiet after all the years of my father's sleeping racket.

That morning she came and sat on the edge of my bed the way she had a thousand times before in my life. She gave me the news as if she had just come from a hospital deathwatch, as if my father had been ill and in pain and was now finally released from his misery. She whispered, "He's gone. Go start the coffee. I'm going to call Mother."

Before I started the water, I put on my robe and went and stood by my parents' bedroom door, watching him. To be blunt while at the same time running the risk of being thought a cold, heartless girl: I had even less feeling for him dead than alive. For years he had made himself unavailable to me, and so the fact that he was now truly unavailable didn't create a void or fill me with a sense of loss. Nothing of that nature. I didn't think I'd have less of a life with him gone. I knew my mother and I would have more.

She appeared beside me, and after a few minutes of watching the body with me, she said she was going outside to wait for her mother, who was on her way to our house for the first time. The curse of absence was lifted. Later I was told that while my mother was standing out in the yard she spoke with the paper man, who subsequently reported his astonishment that she had made her regular highly critical comments about his lax service while giving not the slightest indication that there was a body in the house. Not realizing that he was considered a strange little man himself, he told everybody on his route: "I always knew the woman was odd."

My grandmother arrived and went right to work. She

covered the windows and mirrors in the bedroom with towels and stopped all the clocks in the house. This sounds as though she may have been bordering on voodoo, but she wasn't. These death rituals had lost any magical associations a hundred years before. By the 1930s one would've been hard-pressed to find anyone, except for some of my grandmother's superstitious patients, who believed that a restless spirit could get trapped in an uncovered mirror and howl in the house forever. That morning, when I asked her why she did these things, she said, "My mother performed this routine, and hers and hers and on back. The same reason I crush eggshells. I know witches don't ride to sea in them and sink ships, but my mother did it, and hers and on and on." She judged the cause of death to be a cerebral hemorrhage, but because my father was a man of standing in our community, the county coroner had to come out and give her diagnosis his blessing. He confirmed that my father had died from exactly that, in the wee hours of the morning. My grandmother said to the coroner, "People like to go then, don't they, George?"

He was sitting at the kitchen table, recording something into his notebook, and he looked up at my grandmother and said, "Tender bonds snap before dawn. Isn't that what they say, Charlie Kate?"

My grandmother nodded and left the room to go wash my father's body.

My mother sat down at the table and asked that a cerebral hemorrhage be described to her in full detail. As was to be understood, the coroner at first balked. He asked my mother if she was sure she wanted to know. She looked him in the eyes and said, "I would not have asked."

With that, he began. My mother cocked her head and toyed with an earring, and any man who didn't know her well would've taken this as a sort of flirtation, a first sign of a new widow's losing her mind. She wasn't flirting. She was listening intently, and that was merely the way she fixed herself to listen. At seeing my mother's beautiful head so slightly bent, her mouth open as it was, the coroner, it seemed to me, suffered a burst of desire to impress her, and I would swear on my father's grave that what the man did not know he made up. He was about to say what generally causes the condition, when my mother cleared her throat, moved forward in her chair, and laid both her hands on the table as if to keep it from rising. She spoke as if she were reading from a medical textbook: "It is a condition caused by ingrown selfishness."

After the funeral my mother locked herself in her room and read. My grandmother and I sat in the living room and made excuses for her. Lucky for us (a horrible way to put it), another person in the community died suddenly that same day, and so we were relieved of a long afternoon filled with small talk and strangers. The undertaker took the telephone call in our kitchen and then made the announcement in a maddening fashion that made women remember for years afterward how they had longed to strangle him. He asked for silence while he delivered the news. He said, "There has been another sudden and unfortunate death, one that will touch each of you in a profound way." He did not name the person, and for some time it did not appear that he would. When he was asked to please identify the deceased, he patted his hand in the air and continued with how grieved and so forth we all would be. One woman, who had already started to cry, asked if it was Mr. Roosevelt. He assured her it was not. We all expressed our relief, and then he carried on. My mother had been listening to all this from her bedroom. When she'd heard all she was going to, she shouted, "Jesus! How about just telling who it is! The suspense may kill everybody who's left!"

He was as startled as he should've been, and barely got out the name of Ida's mother, Maureen O'Shea, before he found his hat and left. It took several calls for me to find out the details, and when I told the group what I had learned, the reaction was unanimous: The guilty will not go unpunished. Mrs. O'Shea suffered a miserable choking death in the café in the basement of the courthouse. Reporters covering a murder trial covered her death during their lunch break. When the story appeared in the newspaper, mention was made of the similar fate of her child. The reporter didn't discuss justice and retribution, and he didn't say this death was more proof, as if any of us needed more proof, that the mills of the gods grind slowly but exceeding small. I wondered how many people read the article and then went to bed that evening thinking about horses they had whipped, stray cats they had kicked, and wives they had wounded. I wondered how people slept at all, dreading what was to become of them in the end.

My mother and grandmother and I worked the next week boxing my father's belongings. Although we got everything, down to his key chain, packed and taped up, we couldn't rid the house of the echo of my parents' voices sounding off the walls for too many years, always asking the same question: Is there anybody here who loves me? The three of us put the boxes in the attic. My mother stood on the top step and took boxes that I handed up to her, and she pushed them across the attic floor, grunting each time she shoved a particularly heavy one. When we were through, she backed down the ladder and folded it up into the ceiling. "That's it," she said. "He's all up there." Then she wiped her face and neck with her handkerchief and said, "I have to get out of this house."

She said this with such emphasis that I understood she didn't want to get out of the house for only a few minutes or even a few hours. She wanted to linger somewhere and then come back home restored. I suggested that we go to the beach. My mother considered this for a moment and then thanked me for having such a grand idea. I was very pleased with myself.

My grandmother had never been to the ocean although it was only four hours away by automobile. In her mind, there was nothing to do there but walk and sit, and anyway, she believed she knew exactly what she'd see. When my mother invited her to come with us, she said, "There is nothing but water and sand there, and people aimlessly walking. I have things to do at home."

My mother urged her to set work aside for a few days, saying she could sit in a camp chair and read a favorite collection of shipwreck stories. She told her, "I know you would have a fine time. Please come."

My grandmother thought about this. She must've been seeing herself on the water's edge reading *The Graveyard of the Atlantic*. Then she said, "I guess it would be a shame to die without seeing it." She did not mean this in self-pity, but her regret at having lived so long without seeing so much of the world seemed clear to me. I was soon to learn that it was my vision that had been bordered, not hers.

We left the following morning. We stopped to eat sandwiches wrapped in wax paper at a roadside picnic table, and stuck our heads out of the windows to smell the salt air. When we got to Morehead City, we didn't go to our hotel first but directly to the ocean. My mother and I walked beside my grandmother over the wide strip of sand down to the water. She proceeded across like a camel in her brown high-top shoes from the last century while my mother and I held each other up in our dime-store sandals. She stopped just short of the water, and when we caught up to her, I asked, "So tell me, what do you think of the ocean?"

She stared out over the water and replied without looking at me, "It's fine, but it's actually not as big as I thought it would be."

I asked her if she was disappointed, and she smiled over her shoulder at my mother and me and said, "Only slightly, just the palest disappointment. I thank you both for bringing me."

My mother followed her mother's line of vision, and then mine merged with theirs, and for a second I wondered what we three were supposed to be looking at or looking for.

My grandmother said, "Europe is coming to a rolling boil. Once it starts, it'll take years to finish. Watch and see."

This was August 1936. Two years later, when she and I sat in the movie theater and heard Neville Chamberlain speak of "peace in our time," and then again when we listened to the reports about Poland the following year, and yet again when I was seventeen, listening to reports of Pearl Harbor and Mr. Roosevelt's speech the following day, I heard my grandmother's voice and saw her in her wind-whipped dress and resolute shoes, standing on the edge of her unsatisfactory ocean.

We spent the night at the Atlantis, the only hotel my grandmother would consider. She said she'd be less likely to have a transient drag her out of bed and cut her throat at a place that advertised in *The New Yorker*. It made no difference to her that F. Scott Fitzgerald had a favorite oceanfront room, or that the first palm heart salad seen in North Carolina was served there, or that General Pershing maintained a summer suite there and held court in the manner of General MacArthur years later at the Waldorf-Astoria in New York. All that mattered was the postage-stamp–size advertisement in *The*

New Yorker. We checked into the hotel after our walk on the beach and a flounder dinner at a place called the Sanitary Fish Market, a worrisome name for a restaurant. The hotel lobby was packed with people who had spilled out of the ballroom. A debutante party was in full tilt. Everyone there was dancing and, as far as we could tell, also very drunk. While my mother was checking us in, my grandmother edged her over with her shoulder and told the clerk to tell the debutantes to stop it. They were too loud, and it was time to go to bed. The clerk said he'd see what he could do, which meant he'd do absolutely nothing and take the chance that she'd complain to the management and receive a nice note and a fruit basket as compensation. That my grandmother could think for a second that her command would be heeded and she would stop debutantes from jitterbugging was evidence that she was not fully aware that we lived in a new age in which ladies were not always obeyed and in which turning a profit was worth much more than the patronage of a few people who liked things quiet.

Not only did the music not stop, but we had other accompaniment in the room next door to ours. We complained, got the note and the fruit basket, complained again after midnight and got our room for free. There seemed to be no hope of sleeping, so we sat on one of the beds and played spades. As for next door, this is what happened: A couple entered their room, very full of commotion. I gathered that they had drunk themselves into a near stupor downstairs and had ridden the elevator up mauling each other. They spent several minutes unlocking the door. I heard the girl giggle and bounce down on the bed, and then I heard the boy's shoes drop on the floor. I was afraid of what I'd hear next. My mother pronounced what was going on next door to be more interesting than our game of spades, so she laid down her cards and listened closely. My grandmother and I did the same thing. The boy said at one point, "I'm going to make it so hot in here you'll think two cats have their tails tied together." Then came the mushing around, with most of the noise on his part, and next I listened to all the thousand things he said to try to get the girl to say she loved him. He said over and over, "I hope nobody ever steals you from me. I hope nobody ever steals you."

The girl giggled some more and said, "Who said I was yours? Who said? Jesus, do tell!"

Without warning, my grandmother walked to the adjoining wall, knocked on it hard, and shouted, "She might not be yours now, but she will be in the morning. Get it over with and let me sleep. Hurry up and be quiet!" We heard not another word, moan, giggle, or stir from them.

BIT BY BIT, my grandmother moved in with us. After we returned from the beach, she would spend one night a week, and then two a week and so forth, until, by the late autumn of 1936, she was fully established in our home. Her medical journals and mail-order novels covered every flat surface in the house, except for the kitchen counters, which were jammed with bottles of tonic, jars of salve, and in the middle of all this, a battered, silver-fished herb bible bound with rawhide. It looked to have survived a fire or two. The first job my grandmother gave me was to copy its contents into a new notebook before the bible finished disintegrating, taking a hundred years' worth of curative memories with it.

From the first day she was with us, my eyes stayed wide open in astonishment. I was continuously full of looking, because not only did she come, but her thriving medical practice came with her. Although I had been out on many house calls with her and opened her door to many Saturday-morning patients, nothing could compare with having the afflicted beat their paths across our yard, past my bicycle and old tire swing, up the steps I sat and shelled peas on, through the screen door into the kitchen. And they came right away. She had left a sign on her door notifying patients that she had moved, asking them to pass word to friends and family. I answered the door for the first patient, who said, "Little girl, can you see if Miss Charlie Kate would take a look at me?" I didn't think of myself as a little girl, and if he hadn't looked so desperate for help, I might have told him that I was a young woman now and I was memorizing "Christabel," shaving unseen parts of my legs in secret, and attending romantic movies with my mother. Instead, I ran yelling for my grandmother. I told her a man was at the door who was covered in angry sores and wet blisters.

She trotted to the door. This is what she did for him: She had him sit in our dining room while she boiled every root known to man in my mother's large cast-iron pot, and then she commanded him to drink the potion. He said a little verse from Ezekiel over the cup before he downed it. When he finished, she fixed him another cup, and then gave him a tube of zinc oxide and told him to smear it liberally over every inch of himself. She said, "I would rub it on you only if I were insane." My mother came in from the grocery store while my grandmother was packing leftover pieces of root in her black bag. I was sitting at the other end of the dining room table watching this poor man, listening to him talk about the Millennium, which he was convinced would come in 1955. How far away that year sounded! Just as he was speaking of graves gaping open to release souls to the clouds, I heard my mother shout, "What? A leper? Holy Jesus!" She came into the dining room, yanked me away from the table, and made me stay in my room until he was gone. I remember I was highly disappointed. (I have to say that the pot made everything taste like poison and was put on the porch to be planted with begonias the following spring. Strange to tell, but they thrived and were the envy of all.)

The leper had walked to our house from the Outer Banks, where he worked as a jackleg mechanic on fishing boats. He must have made his way to Wake County and then begun asking for directions to Miss Charlie Kate's. Although most people would assume that by this time all the remaining lepers in the world had been collected into colonies in India or in the big leprosarium in Louisiana, this was not the case, not in actuality. They were reported to roam much in the manner of gypsies and were sighted usually toward the wild, farther reaches of the coast where the famous Lost Colony became—not meaning to sound funny—lost.

. My grandmother was proud that her reputation was so widespread as to have reached a fishing boat mechanic on the Outer Banks. Later in her life, when a newspaper reporter annoyed her with questions about her nonexistent official credentials, she asked him, "When was the last time anybody walked a hundred miles, scabbed and blistered, seeking your advice and authority?" This leper was thereafter referred to as our first emergency patient, but before long, other cases came. However, I will say that none was ever as exotic in a biblical sort of way as the leper. The lame and toothachy and headachy quickly learned she was there, and presented themselves at our door. All these pained people would call through the screen, "Little girl, can you please fetch Miss Charlie Kate for me?" Women in despair over colicky babies came, it seemed, in droves. These women were always young, usually pale and limp, always poor and apologetic for having nothing to offer my grandmother in payment except things like pretty conch shells or old stockings and, once, a promise of changing the sick baby's name to Charlie Kate. I remember my grandmother's prescription for these screaming babies: "Say a prayer, and turn your baby heels up and head down three times an hour. Put seven knots in a string and tie it loose around her middle, and leave it there until it rots off. Give a little water on the hour hand and let her eat after you eat. Walk away from strong root foods like turnips and onions—do not even smell the pot boiling. In between feeding her, sit in a straight chair with her across your knees, head down, looking at the floor. Keep a trifling bounce steady. Your knees will feel good to her gassiness. She'll go to sleep for nothing to look at but the floor. Anybody would."

If no calls came in for a day or two, my grandmother would become restless. She would jump up from reading and announce, "I'm going to *find* somebody." Then she would drive downtown to City News and Candy because she knew the place would be full of patients. The town's living dead accumulated there. They sat around on old automobile seats and spat in a brass spittoon that they passed around

like a collection plate. This place sold every magazine and
newspaper in the world, although nobody ever bought much
of anything except lawyers from down at the courthouse,
who liked to go about with *The New York Times* folded
under their arms. It was actually an outlet for bootleg gin,
which accounted for the constant feeling of destitution and
fatigue, all these tired hearts waiting for the next shipment
to arrive. Despite the gloomy atmosphere, I loved to accom-
pany my grandmother there. A true joy in my life was the
sight of her outside my school, waiting for me, calling out the
car window, "Don't get on the bus! Ride with me to the
News and Candy!" She always let me fill a small sack with
hard candy while she bought a *New Yorker* and a *Saturday
Review of Literature*. Then she would range around, from
one old alcoholic to another, shaking hands, asking after
spouses in her usual way: not "How is the wife?" but "Is she
dead yet?" None of the old men seemed startled or offended
by this. Their answers were mainly that the wife was near
death, or that she had just died and they had been getting
along fairly poorly since. And then somebody would ask,
"Can you take a look at me?" My grandmother would
answer, "I just came to get a magazine, but I guess I could."
She would ask me to trot out to the car to get her bag, acting
as if it were so very lucky that she happened to have it. If
the men had known she had come specifically for them, they
might not have come forward so easily.

The place became something of a waiting room for the
chronically pathetic. Men bared gums and asked her to
comment on abscesses. They asked her to diagnose the

causes of swollen feet, tongues, fingers, noses, everything on a body that could swell. One man proclaimed, "I am swollen in general." Another said, "I want you to pronounce on a blood blister, if you would be so kind." Still another man bared his chest and displayed a mysterious rash shaped like the star of Bethlehem, and when my grandmother asked him how long he had had this, he told her he had been born with it, but that didn't mean he liked it. He wanted it taken off. She told him he had lived with the rash seventy years and could live with it another ten, and so he buttoned up his shirt and that was that. She would always glance into the spittoon, and if something worrisome was in it, she'd say, "Who spit out these coffee grounds?" Whoever confessed would be sent to Mary Elizabeth's Hospital with a note for the radiologist to run barium tests at my grandmother's expense.

Stomach ulcers were the predominant ailment among these men, living as they did on gin, cigarettes, and candy. My grandmother would take men into the storage room and view cases of piles and hernias and, once, a case of inflamed testicles that caused a man to disregard my presence and say, "Charlie Kate, my privates are on fire." While she was in there, I would sit and look at magazines and listen to the inevitable murmurs of memory that arose as soon as the door to the storage room was closed: "Remember the time Charlie Kate sewed Licky Smith on her table, and how he came back to work fat and happy and so proud of his red thread? Remember when she went to that girl's house who spent all one Easter Sunday jumping off the porch trying to

63

get rid of her baby, and how she tied her hands and feet to the porch rail and made her watch her neighbor playing with her children in her yard? Remember when she got Tessa Jerrod's arm out of the wringer? I was there. She unplugged the machine and it still didn't let her go, and Charlie Kate said, 'By God, I am telling you to let this woman's arm loose!' The wringer widened and out flopped Tessa's arm, flat as a breadboard. Everybody there, like me, who had come running on account of Tessa's screaming, felt the Holy Spirit in the wash shed. Rosalinda Herbert's neuralgia was healed on the spot. Amos Johnson's hair started to grow. Buttercup Spivey's dropped kidneys rose. Malcolm Taylor stopped wanting to scratch his missing leg. Everybody saw the miracles all around."

More than once, she told the men as she was packing her bag to leave, "I will remind every one of you that a drunkard makes an ugly corpse." They would cock their heads and regard her words like a bunch of scholars who had just heard something wise and true, and never before considered.

My grandmother's grand reputation was made more so by, of all people, the real doctor who had earlier sent her ten dollars. He caused marvelous opportunities to come her way after she told him she knew of his grave and shameful error. One night in January of 1937 she was called out to the long row of mill houses on Beale Street to treat a tiny blind baby racked with whooping cough. My mother and I went with her and took turns jumping out of the automobile to run ahead and salt icy patches on the road to town. We sat in the backseat with a large bag of salt between us, and when my grandmother stopped, predicting a slick place ahead, one of us would scoop into the bag with a measuring cup and then hop out. We did this because the chains for the tires had been stolen from our garage, along with tools, old toys, anything that could be traded for food or whiskey at the Hooverville by the railroad yard.

I knew that my mother had grown up in this mill section, but I had difficulty imagining her running about, playing with these ragged children who were still outside in the raw cold of midnight, chasing each other up and down the street with icicle daggers. As we walked up the steps and into the sick baby's house, I heard her shrieking, but that was the only sound. It seemed so very strange to me, and then I realized that between the sharp cries I was not hearing a mother saying everything would be all right. There was no mothering sound.

The mother looked to be my age. She stood holding the baby in the middle of a room that might have been a pretty little space the first fifteen minutes it was in use. But now the stains on the walls had stains, and the one electric bulb overhead dangled like something one would expect to see in a cell on death row. She was doing such a useless job of comforting the baby that she may as well have laid her in her crib to scream alone and walked out. My grandmother said to her very directly, "Give me the baby." She took her to the settee to examine her abdomen. I was asked to come hold the baby's legs still. They were jerking violently up into her chest, and although she was only about two years old, she seemed to have in her legs the power of five grown men.

My mother went out to the car and brought in four wooden poles and one of the bronchitis tents we always packed when a case of whooping cough was suspected. The tents were nothing more than sheets, but my mother had embroidered baby animals on them, so a sick and miserable child could have some sort of pleasure. During that bad winter and early spring, thirty or forty children used this tent. After my mother constructed the tent over the crib, she sat down with the young woman and took the baby's medical history, which proceeded along a string of "I don't know" and "I can't remember" until the question of the baby's blindness arose. My mother asked if she had been born that way.

The baby's mother said, "The doctor, he caught her and then he put the drops in and sort of spilled some on her and I sort of got the feeling he did it."

My grandmother had placed the baby on her stomach, and I was still holding the legs. She was on her knees by the settee, with one ear pressed into the baby's back. The windowpanes rattled with the child's screaming, but my grandmother heard the young woman's response, lifted her head from the baby's back, and asked, "Did he say anything to you?"

The young woman nodded. "Yes ma'am. He said, 'Damn it all to hell.' "

My grandmother didn't ask anything else. My mother stopped her questioning as well and went into the kitchen and started in on the considerable stack of dishes. The young woman didn't stop her.

When my mother and I went out on house calls, we usually walked into a mess, though never one as severe as this, and part of our duty was to clean. My grandmother asked me to boil a croup kettle and to heat the plaster she had brought already mixed, and while I stood stirring at the stove, trying to keep the plaster from sticking to the pan, she walked up and down the room with the baby. The young woman stood with her back against the wall, looking at the three of us as if we were taking over her life. She seemed indifferent to it. When the plaster was warm enough, my grandmother spread the mixture on a width of torn sheet and swaddled and pinned the baby up in the wrapping like a little cocoon. As she did this, she asked where the baby's father was.

The young woman said, "He's drunk."

My grandmother said, "Drunk is not a place. Where is he?"

The young woman said he was at a pool parlor in an even worse part of town than this one. My grandmother told my mother and me to go home and to return with food and more medicine the next day. We went out to the automobile and brought in the satchel of extra clothes she kept in the trunk during whooping cough season, and then we went home, stopping as we had done before to salt the icy places. My grandmother stayed in that house with the blind baby and her washed-out mother and her hard-drinking father for two nights and three days, administering half a grain of antipyrine to the child every few hours. She never left anybody alone who was taking this drug. When she finally returned home, she fixed herself up on a little laudanum and slept like a bear, on top of her covers with all her clothes on.

The next afternoon she emptied out a startling handful of suma, for energy, and sarsaparilla, for courage and vigor, swallowed them without water, and then dictated a letter for my mother to take down, addressed to the real doctor. My mother used her best linen stationery and her best Palmer penmanship. In this letter my grandmother called him a thug, a hoodlum, a coward, and an overall disgrace to their profession. She suggested that the baby be afforded every future comfort that a blind child could have, including but not limited to entry into the Governor Morehead School for the Blind. She suggested that an account be set up in the mother's name at the general store nearest her home and that all bootleggers in the region be put on notice to deny the father alcohol under penalty of having their livelihoods exposed and their families ruined.

The doctor wrote her back a tortured and near incoherent letter in which he confessed to having spilled silver nitrate in the baby's eyes. He said he despised himself and deserved to die, things of that nature. He consented to everything my grandmother suggested, and then swore to do all he could to advance her career. He wasn't kidding. The next week things started happening for her. She was appointed to the War Orphan Board, the State Committee on

Inter-racial Cooperation, and the Rural Midwifery Council. She was given a lifetime subscription to *The New England Journal of Medicine* as well as permission to have her patients' prescriptions filled at Hayes Barton Pharmacy. She wanted one more thing, which, however, would always be denied: the power to admit patients into Mary Elizabeth's Hospital. The doctor did, though, promise to admit her cases on his authority. My mother asked her how she could take things from this doctor, and my grandmother said, "Nothing is happening I do not already deserve and have not deserved for some time."

But an achievement some months afterward that won her a feature interview in the Sunday paper as well as a bio-graphical sketch in the next year's edition of *Busy North Carolina Women* had nothing to do with the real doctor's gratitude. She single-handedly saved five children in a back-woods family from malaria. She was called to the family's home, a filthy cabin on a stagnant loop of the Tar River, on the evening of the Fourth of July. She had just walked back in from reprimanding our neighbor's four children for ex-ploding firecrackers underneath a tin tub, when Marvin Jenkins, a tall, oafish boy who came to school every three months or so, banged up the steps and shouted through the screen door into the kitchen, "I've come for the doctor! Come on! Everybody's going to be dead! Mama said tell you they're too hot!"

We knew the boy was talking about malaria, because it had been a dangerously hot summer, and we knew where and how his family lived. Every once in a while malaria roared through the lower-lying areas of this part of the state, and those with a mind to helping themselves as God commanded had long since moved to higher ground. This particular family was of the variety made famous in *Tobacco Road,* so one fairly easily gets the point that they suffered everything from close-breeding to ticks. My grandmother loaded her satchel, cursing the fact that she had only two quinine tablets left. Knowing she was useless sick, she swallowed them and said she would send out for more once she got to the boy's house, and realizing the trip there would be a muddy ordeal for her, my mother and I wanted to go with her, even without quinine, but she assured us that she would be fine.

When she walked past us, we noticed her shoes were missing the laces. "They're soaking," she said. "I'll keep my toes bunched." The laces were soaking, as they were every Sunday night, in a bowl of linseed oil. By doing this, she had made them last thirty years. "My shoestrings," she told me once, "have lasted years longer than most people can stand each other." As we watched her climb into the rickety buggy, my mother said how worried she was that the boy wouldn't get my grandmother to his house before dark. There was to be no moon that night, and nights on the back loop of the river were said to be darker than black, darker than the Earl of Hell himself.

My grandmother had to help the boy dig the buggy out of the river mud twice. They didn't get to his house until after ten o'clock. She went right in and immediately confirmed five roaring cases of malaria. She had left so hurriedly that she forgot her prescription pad. When she searched the

Jenkins house for a piece of paper, she found nothing. She told me later, "I looked up and I looked down, and then I looked up and I looked down again. The mother of this gang told me they never had a call for paper, and whenever they got any it was highly appreciated in the outbuilding." What did my grandmother do? She wrote out a lengthy prescription on the side frame of the bedroom door and instructed the oldest boy to rip the piece of wood off the wall and take it to Hayes Barton and wake up the pharmacist, who lived over the store. While the boy was gone, she chastised the mother for keeping her children in a filthy hotbox, and then sent another boy to our house to collect clean linens.

The five children survived, though sorry to tell, they didn't amount to anything worthy of the heroic effort that had been put forth to save their lives.

I kept the newspaper photograph of these recuperating children, all of them sitting up in one bed with the famous door frame displayed across their legs. For years, the piece of wood hung over the soda fountain at the Hayes Barton Pharmacy, where I ate lunch every day. On a particularly lonesome anniversary of my grandmother's death I decided the frame was mine, and I crawled up among the milk shake machines and juice presses, took it down, and carried it home. The sympathetic old pharmacist, full of memory as he was, let me go without a word. I marched home down Glenwood Avenue with it underneath my arm, in a frenzy of relentless grief.

My grandmother had been with us for two years when her life changed. One afternoon she, my mother, and I were hanging out laundry in our backyard. The week before, Maveen had told us, "I feel too old to work," and had gone to the next county to live with her sister. It was a perfect day for drying laundry, a day with a hot, stern wind. That was as much as we were discussing. For some reason, I felt compelled to look across the wide cotton field by our house. It meant looking directly into the sun, but I did it anyway. And there, on the edge of the field, was an old man, suitcase in hand. I knew in my heart he had not been there two seconds before. He had appeared to me perfectly at once, as if he had been dropped standing upright from the clouds. I told my mother and grandmother to look at him. He was so still, staring at us. My grandmother looked up from the clothes basket, and without a word she started to run for him. At fifty-six, she ran to him like a young girl. He had given her nothing except sadness for so many years, but as I watched her fly into his arms, my thought was this: Oh, how she loves him is untelling.

He acted like the stranger he was. He was cordial to my mother, cordial to me, and one would've thought he'd have brought us presents, but he didn't. He drank our coffee and ate everything in the house while my mother stood by the kitchen sink, regarding him and the way he ate without stopping. He looked to be all gristle, and he smelled—to be blunt—of bourbon and urine. My grandmother began pouring on the coffee and the charm. She seemed to have come completely out of herself. It was startling. After he swore on the Holy Bible that he could not eat another bite, he asked my mother what time the next bus for Raleigh drove by our house. She told him, and my grandmother said, "In that case, I'd better get ready."

She packed all her necessities with great speed, standing at the dresser and tossing garments into the open satchel on her bed. My mother asked her in a thousand different ways if she knew what she was doing. My grandmother kept saying she was in a hurry and could not talk. I went back into the kitchen and watched this man, this grayed and stinking man, and convinced myself that he looked like the sort of man who wouldn't mind answering a personal question.

I said, "Excuse me, but you know, my mother is pretty shaken up by all this. Can you please tell me what you're doing here?"

He said, "She doesn't look upset to me. She looks fine. I just came back to get Charlie Kate."

I told him my mother didn't show these things, but I knew her well enough to know how she felt.

He said, "You can get in a world of trouble reading minds. It is a truly hazardous hobby." Then he wanted to know if I could wrap up the rest of our delicious pineapple cake in some wax paper for him and his bride to enjoy at the hotel.

A few minutes before the bus was due to pass by, we all went outside, and when we saw the top of it in the distance, shining like a new dime, my grandfather walked into the middle of the road and stood there, looking ready to be run over. He glanced back over his shoulder at my mother, who was jiggled up tight with alarm and fury, and he said, "Sugar, I mean not to miss this bus."

My grandmother wasn't a hugger, so the fact that she boarded the bus to Raleigh without so much as giving us a peck on the cheek did not hurt our feelings. The bus hissed and pulled away and left my mother and me standing in our front yard, not knowing whether we were supposed to wave them off, or stand there and cry, or what. We went back inside and asked each other for the rest of the day if what had just happened had truly happened. If we had not re-membered the laundry outside, all the wet things we'd left to sour in the basket, we would have had nothing to do but sit and wonder. My mother said, "Thank God for laundry." We rewashed everything left in the basket, so grateful to have something to do with our hands.

We did not hear anything from my grandmother for three days. Then the phone rang at four o'clock in the morning.

My grandmother shouted, "Margaret? Margaret?"

I shouted back, "Where are you?"

She told me she was at the Sir Walter Hotel, which was the best place in town, and she would be waiting out front for us to come pick her up right away. Then she hung up. I awakened my mother, and she got dressed, and off we went. From five blocks away, we could see my grandmother on the sidewalk. We pulled up beside her and jumped out and rushed at her, asking what was wrong, was she hurt, things of that nature. She said she was not hurt, and without another word she opened the back door and crawled onto the seat.

As we drove back home, my mother tried again and again to make her tell us what was going on. My grandmother said it was none of our business. When my mother would not stop, she sighed and said, "Well, if it'll make you be quiet, I'll tell you."

My mother said, "That would be nice."

My grandmother opened her black satchel and pulled out a great power of money, a gangster wad actually. She held it up to my mother's face and said, "You see this? This is your father's. Or it *was* his. It's mine now."

My mother shouted, "You mean you *rolled* him?"

My grandmother said, "If that means I let him take what he wanted and then I took what I wanted, I suppose I did."

I had to know, so I asked my grandmother how much she had there, and she said, "Four-fifty, six, six-fifty, seven . . ." She licked her finger and counted the last few bills silently and then said, "One thousand three hundred and sixty-five dollars, to be exact." Then she stuck the wad back into her satchel, snapped the huge clasp, and that was that.

My mother asked her what she intended to do with it and, more important, what she was going to do when he came after it.

My grandmother said, "I don't know and I don't know. I'm tired. Wake me when we're home."

Later I learned that she donated all this money to the Confederate Ladies' Home, where three of my mother's spinster teachers from Miss Nash's School were spending their last years penniless, playing an endless game of bridge in a dank parlor, wearing cameo chokers and little spots of rouge in the middle of their cheeks. She wrote very specific instructions for the disbursement of the money. It was to be used to buy a seven-tube radio, a new Victrola, magazine subscriptions galore, leather-bound editions of Shakespeare, Tolstoy, Hardy, and Dickens. She also included writers of the South, but not Thomas Wolfe, whose style addled her to distraction even though she took his part in the debate over *Look Homeward, Angel.* Whatever was left was to be used for group trips to Charleston and Savannah. It appeared as though she meant to liven the place up. I wish I knew whether she succeeded. I like to think she did.

As for my grandfather's coming after any of this money: He knew better. We never heard from him again.

My grandmother had run to him so convincingly. Love seemed to be screaming out as she ran, or maybe, since love and revenge grow from the same kernel of want, I was mistaken. She could've been hoarding a dream of vengeance for more than twenty years, and that run was part of the plan. Or the run may have been true, and the reality of starting her life over with a stinking, old, untrustworthy man hit her as she watched him gum his food in the best room in town. She may have looked at him sleeping and despised him for leaving her, after all those lovely times he had carried her back and forth across the river on his barge, leading her to believe that she would always be cared for so sweetly. I wondered what they said to each other in the room, what they did for each other until that moment when my grandmother decided the man had had use of her heart long enough.

A WOMAN telephoned our house for my grandmother about six months after she abandoned my grandfather at the Sir Walter Hotel. She took the receiver, listened a few minutes, and then said to the person on the other end, "I imagined you would be dead." She listened a little more and asked, "Did he purge?"

The woman was an old family acquaintance my grandmother had not seen or heard from in years, and was calling to tell her that my grandfather had passed away at her home earlier that day. My grandmother motioned for a pen and paper to be brought to her, and she wrote down the funeral arrangements, such as they were. When she was off the phone, she turned to my mother and said, "Your father died. We need to go to Pasquotank County tomorrow." She gave no indication of wanting to talk about it further, and went to the stove to make tea.

My mother's eyes filled quickly, and she dabbed them dry

with a dish towel. She said to her mother, "I heard you ask if he purged. Did he?"

My grandmother stopped midway to the sink with the teakettle and looked out the window, out toward the spot where we had seen him standing, and sighed and said, "Yes, he did."

The fact that he had foamed at the mouth immediately upon dying indicated that he had had a great backjam of wishes and desires and truths that were never spoken. His love for his wife and child and his remorse over having left them were expressed, at the end, in spite of himself. Out bubbled all the words he had swallowed while he was alive. My grandmother put aside everything she knew about the automatic reactions of bodies in order to hear a dead man say that he was sorry.

I said, "Suppose he hadn't purged?"

My mother spoke for the two of them. "We would've sold him to the medical school in Chapel Hill and let them do as they pleased with him."

The next day the three of us went to Pasquotank County. He was laid out at the home of the friend who had called. Besides the woman, who was wearing a thin dress without a much-needed brassiere, the only person there was my grandfather's uncle. He was the oldest person I had ever seen. He had lived on the Pasquotank next to my grandparents. My mother acted genuinely happy to see him, but my grandmother ignored him.

When my mother asked her why she couldn't say just a couple of words to Uncle Otha, she was told, "He does not exist."

My mother asked, "Still?"

My grandmother said, "Yes. I have not forgotten, and never will."

Later in the day, I asked my mother about this and was told that the man had once stolen five dollars from my grandmother and then lied about it. "If he had only stolen from her," she said, "she'd at least act like he was in the room."

I mentioned how very old he looked. My mother told me he was probably well over a hundred, and although he was repugnant to her mother, she held fond childhood memories of him. She and I were sitting on the back steps of the old woman's house, sneaking a cigarette together. She said, "He was at Shiloh and loved to tell about it, although the people he told couldn't bear it because it broke their hearts in a million places. But I thrived on hearing about it, so he talked to me continuously. Listen to this. He took a bullet in the head, and the doctors in the field got it out, cleaned the wound, and then took a silver dollar and mashed it into this thin sliver and put it in the place in his head. Isn't that wonderful?"

She had always been drawn to horror tales, ghost stories, and real-life accounts of the weird and unusual. Her curious nature and her mother's profession made this more or less unavoidable. She was going through a phase of addiction to magazines like *True Crime* and *Weird Tales and Startling Adventures,* and right before this trip she had come into my room, awakened me, and read aloud a story about Bonnie and Clyde and how they were blown all apart, their limbs and things then preserved and later basted together in some slaphappy fashion. Curiosity-seekers apparently lined up to see all this, and one man who was interviewed said he would've readily paid money for the privilege, as would have my mother. She asked me as she did with regard to Uncle Otha's head, "Isn't that wonderful?" I said it was not. I said it was gruesome, and I thanked her in advance for my nightmares. She argued that it was an example of the marvelous extremes present in human nature, and thus began an argument that made me too tired to sleep. That is why I let the silver dollar in the man's head pass as wonderful. I never possessed her stamina for debate.

When we went back inside we saw that four pallbearers and a preacher had arrived, ready to do their business. They all expected to be paid for their services, and my grandmother was expected to pay them. She said she had no intention of doing this, and so she asked my mother to ask Otha if he had any money with him.

My mother said, "Why don't you ask him yourself?"

My grandmother said, "In my eyes, he does not exist."

I asked my mother how much money she had, and she asked me the same. Between us we had sixty cents.

My mother looked at the old family friend in her too thin dress and red lipstick, and said, "What about you?"

She said, "I'm broke. He ate up every penny I had."

My grandmother pointed first to the coffin and then to the woman and said, "You know, if a woman's husband comes to your house to pleasure himself and then dies, I'd think you could at least split the cost of the arrangements with his widow."

The old woman pled poverty again, and my grandmother said, "That's okay. Give me that clock on the mantel, and I'll give these fellows fifty cents each and the preacher a dollar." The clock was taken from the mantel and handed to my grandmother in the calm manner of all rituals. She carried it as we walked the short way to the cemetery. I still can see her walking along the narrow path through the meadow, holding time against her breast like a baby.

My mother asked her what she planned to do with herself now that she was officially a widow. She had asked the question in a lighthearted, teasing manner, but my grandmother didn't respond in the same spirit.

She said, "What makes you think I'd want a man now? I'd take a poison pill before I'd take a man." Then she told my mother it was rude and maybe even bad luck to talk nonsense on the way to a grave.

My grandfather wasn't so much buried as he was put in the ground. After the preacher finished his dollar prayer, he tried to console my grandmother, who told him, "I don't want to hear it." The three of us started back across the meadow without saying much of a good-bye to anyone, except that my mother hugged Otha, who told her he expected to be dead before the end of the year.

He was, too. We heard through another phone call from the same old woman. My grandmother said to her again, "I imagined you would be dead." Then she listened a moment and said, "No, I don't care to come see him buried. You know he did not exist for me. How many does this make now?" She listened again and said, "You may not think it's your fault, but you get a man in there with a bad heart and do all these things to him, and there he goes. You've been doing this for fifty years, you'd think you'd find one with a dime to leave you. You're stupider than I thought you were." She hung up the phone, looked at me, and said, "I'd rather you wash chamber pots the rest of your life than conduct business on your back."

On the way home from Pasquotank County that afternoon, we passed the path that led through the woods to the home of Maveen's sister. We turned around and drove down the path, talking all the way of how good it would be to see her. We had not hired a replacement. We had tried, but my grandmother turned candidates away midway through the interviews. When one after another of them was out the door, she would say, "I found her lacking." After she did this five or six times, my mother gave up and announced that we would cook and clean for ourselves. The three of us cooked and ate like bachelors, and the only real challenge with our laundry was soaking blood out of garments.

Maveen's sister let us in. She didn't greet us as much as grab and pull us through the long hall, saying, "I should've sent for you. I should've." When she opened the door to Maveen's tiny room, we saw the reason she was so alarmed. The room reeked of vomit. Maveen was asleep on her side, facing us, her mouth white-rimmed with bicarbonate. She looked to weigh sixty pounds. She had been a large, strong woman, raw-boned. My mother asked what was wrong with her, and her sister said, "She screamed for two weeks and then slacked off, and now something's in her eating all her food, at least what doesn't come back up. Whatever it is won't let her have enough to eat. They say it's tapeworm indigestion."

My grandmother asked, "Who is *they?*"

Maveen's sister said, "Mr. Roosevelt's crowd." By this, she meant one of the public health clinics that had been established in county seats.

My grandmother went over, leaned down, and gently ran her hands over Maveen's stomach, palpating her as best she could through three layers of calico. Then she laid a hand on her forehead, frowning all the while, and when she stood up she said she would be back the next morning. She told Maveen's sister to stop giving her bicarbonate or solid food and to strip her down and rub her with alcohol every three hours. My grandmother left quickly, my mother and I following at a trot. If we had not been able to keep pace with her, I believe, we would've been left. My grandmother was thoroughly preoccupied. As soon as the car doors shut, she told us that Maveen had cancer and would be dead in six weeks. She would starve to death.

We asked my grandmother what she intended to do. She told us she was going to ask the real doctor, the one whose career she had spared, to admit Maveen to the hospital, where she could be more comfortable. When we got back home, my grandmother went right in and called him at his house. She answered his questions calmly at first: "She's seventy. She's lost probably a hundred pounds. Distended abdomen. Temperature of a hundred and three or thereabout. No, no sign of pain now, but I'm sure there's intestinal paralysis. I'm worried about rupture. She's got to be hospitalized right now." When she disagreed with his response, she tried not to shout. She spoke in a high, thin voice. "I don't believe it! It would take nothing for you to do this. You'd better watch out! Soon I might not be the only one around here practicing without a license."

She slammed the phone down, plopped down at the kitchen table, and mimicked him. "The only thing that goes wrong below an old colored woman's waist is fibroids. That, and too much grease. Let's keep on with the bicarbonate."

We went back to Maveen's house the next morning. I remember packing a snack of graham crackers and apple butter and putting a copy of *The Mill on the Floss* in the bag to read if I had any spare time. As it turned out, I had no time to read, and afterward I associated the book so much with Maveen that I could never bear to finish it. When I walked into her room with my grandmother I was startled to see her completely naked body. She lay curled like a baby with her arms up over her head, a bad-luck sleeping position that means a person is calling trouble. In spite of the breeze from the fan, she looked buttered, glistening with sweat. My grandmother checked for dehydration, which was present, and then slipped a thermometer underneath Maveen's arm, and when she read it, she whispered, "Why she's not dead is a mystery." Then she told us we were all going to stay there as long as it took. I asked her how long she thought that might be. She unclipped the railroad watch from her bosom and said, "It's ten o'clock now. Mercy will take her by suppertime." My mother led Maveen's sister, dazed and staggering, from the room.

Maveen held on until nine o'clock that evening. My mother kept her sister in the yard most of the time. I could see them through the bedroom window. My mother had pulled two metal chairs close together, and though I couldn't hear anything, I could see that the sister held a Bible in her lap. Her head was nodding in rhythm to the verses. Under different circumstances my mother would've nitpicked discrepancies and rolled her eyes over the miracles, but on this afternoon she nodded along with Maveen's sister. I stayed inside with my grandmother in the dying light of that old woman's dying day. My grandmother held one of Maveen's hands, and I held the other. She slipped away from us in a manner that I almost want to call graceful, and she purged, not much but some. I put my head on the foot of the bed and cried until the lingering odor of vomit in the sheets made it impossible for me to breathe.

I felt my grandmother's hand on my back. I asked her, "What do you think she meant to say? What do you think were her secret wishes and desires?"

As she covered the body and reached over to stop the clock on the nightstand, and moved about the room, hanging towels on mirrors and glasses, making all her death rounds, she said, "I'm not sure, but it could've been something having to do with a certain useless doctor. I'm thoroughly disgusted. He's blinded one and helped starve another, and that's just the two I know about."

When we left that evening, my grandmother directed my mother to drive to Anderson Heights, a neighborhood of grand houses and fine lawns. In these homes lived Raleigh's chief doctors and lawyers and a dying breed of Southerner, white people who seemed to earn a living automatically. She gave me a street address, and she would not listen to my mother's protests that she couldn't go to anybody's house this late in the evening. My mother asked into the rearview mirror, "What do you want me to do?" She said, "Keep driving. The hour does not faze me." We drove through what felt like a true maze of affluence before we found the right house. My mother and I sat in the car and listened to the radio while my grandmother went up to the house. A butler let her in. I remember my mother's saying, "Remarkable. Truly remarkable. People are hungry three miles from here. A butler. Remarkable." My grandmother stayed in the house about fifteen minutes, and when she returned, all she said was, "I took care of the situation for certain this time."

The next week my mother brought a newspaper article to my attention. She pointed to a picture of a fine-looking gentleman and said, "Isn't that him?"

I said it was. It was the real doctor, and the world, I'm sure, was shocked to learn of his early retirement. My grandmother came in the kitchen and looked over my shoulder at the article.

"What do you think about this?" I asked.

She said, "I think I should have taken him off the streets a long time ago." Then she took down her mortar and pestle, mashed two cloves of garlic, spread the paste on toast, and ate it without blinking.

One morning my mother asked why I wasn't dressed for school. I reminded her that it was the end of a grading period, and students with high averages were allowed to skip the reading day before examinations. She suggested that we go to the movies. She wanted to see *Gone With the Wind*. Because of the movie's grand popularity, the theater stayed so packed in the evenings and on the weekends that a weekday afternoon was the only time she believed we could find three seats together. My grandmother went even though she had disliked the novel and thought the movie could only be worse. My mother and I didn't really care, as we would watch anything all the way through and see it again if it stayed in town long enough. My grandmother would not. If she didn't like a picture, she would get up and leave without a word, and if she had suffered through no more than thirty minutes of the movie she would request, and receive, a refund. She'd sit in the lobby and read until we came out, and if we asked her why she had left, she'd say, "It was stupid" or "I didn't believe any of it."

The only time she ever implored us to leave a movie with her was that afternoon. She leaned forward in the darkness and whispered, "Come on. I'm not going to let you watch this." I mouthed, "Why?" She said, "It's hideous. You'll walk out retarded. Come on."

My mother wouldn't budge. I got up because I didn't like the thought of my grandmother alone in the lobby for two and a half hours. She had forgotten to pack a book in her satchel, so we walked down to the bookseller's and bought *The Yearling* at the clerk's urging. We walked around a bit

and then went back to the theater lobby and read it together. I remember her asking me, "Do you think this is
maudlin?" I told her I did not. She considered my opinion
a moment, grunted, and started back on the page. After a
few minutes, she handed the book to me and said, "You
take it. I can't stand it. Not enough happens." She got up
and said she was going next door to the drugstore to buy a
newspaper, and while she was gone I wondered at all her
complexities and inconsistencies, how she could walk out on
a movie in which everything in the world occurs, and then
dismiss a novel on the grounds that not enough happens.

When my mother emerged squinting from the theater,
she was not alone. She had a man with her. He was of
ordinary height and weight, but unlike the other men in
town, who hadn't been able to buy a new stitch of clothing
since 1928, he was dressed in sharply pleated gabardine
pants, a tweed jacket, a stylish tie, and excellent cordovan
loafers. He walked right up to us with my mother and put
out his hand as she introduced him. "This is Mr. Richard
Baines," she said. "We met during intermission. Where
were you two?"

Shaking this man's hand, I told my mother we had been
down to the bookseller's and must have missed her then. He
shook my grandmother's hand. She looked at him hard
enough for him to understand that a quick explanation was
in order. He told us that he was new in town, and that after
a nice chat with my mother during intermission she was
gracious enough to consent to sit with him for the remainder
of the picture. He looked and sounded as if he already

adored my mother, right down to the ground. My grandmother glared at her, and had she reached over and twisted
her earlobe my mother could not have felt any more chastised. I stood there and made small talk with him and my
mother for a moment, and then suddenly my grandmother
blurted, "Well, Mr. Baines, it was nice to have met you."
We were out of the theater in no time.

All the way to the car and all the way home, my grandmother and mother fought as I had never seen them fight
before. They fixed their theme early and stuck to it: There
is a man lurking. What are we going to do about it? My
grandmother said mainly that my mother didn't need a man,
that she had been happier without one and would *remain*
happy that way. My mother responded with variations of
"What makes you so sure? Haven't you been looking at me
close enough to tell I'm actually lonely?"

She was showing signs of loneliness. She had recently
begun the process of resigning herself to the slide from
beautiful lady to handsome older woman, adjusting her lipstick color from fire-engine red to brick, exchanging bright
beads for pearls and stylish platform soles for pumps. And
by "process," I mean just that; she had not fully committed
her body to middle age yet. There were still her stockings
with the perfect seams that she knew exactly how to reach
down and adjust in a restaurant, making all the men's heads
swivel in such a way that their wives must have said to
themselves, "She's not sixteen anymore. How does she *do*
that?" There were her cheekbones, high as they could be
without disappearing into her eyes. The shadowy hollow of

her cheeks gave her a slightly hungry look, and of all the things she gave me, even the bright beads that I would exchange for her pearls in the coming of my own middle age, I was always most grateful for the cheekbones. There were other signs, seen not so much in her appearance as in her behavior. She hid herself in her room and read romantic stories too much, listened to the radio too much, busied herself with volunteer work too much, blowing arguments with co-workers out of proportion so she would have something to fix her mind on for a day or two. And when I changed her sheets each Monday morning I saw the indisputable evidence of her rising loneliness. She had started going to bed with her makeup on, and then smearing the pillowcase with mascara cried off during the night. Although I had always believed my grandmother to possess the ability to see into, beyond, and through the human heart, she had not seen my mother's loneliness emerging. Even as quietly and slightly as it came, I thought she would have seen it.

My grandmother shouted, "You could've had Charles Nutter when he was offered to you. Now look! You're thirty-five years old. Haven't you learned *anything*?"

My mother wouldn't answer, even though she was probably about to explode with the reply that Charles Nutter hadn't wanted a child bride. She knew my grandmother meant hadn't she learned anything in regard to men and how they would, at best, take advantage of her or, at worst, leave her.

My grandmother said, "Well, if you won't answer that, would you mind at least telling me what he does for a living?"

My mother said she didn't know. He hadn't mentioned it to her.

Under her breath, my grandmother said, "Must not be much." She turned her body toward the window, letting us know the conversation was closed.

My grandmother believed our household was fine as it was. If there was heavy lifting to be done, the three of us did it together. If a picture needed hanging, we tapped the wall to listen for the stud and then drove the nail in with an admirable economy of hits. If anything mechanical broke, for instance the mantel clock from Pasquotank County, we took it apart on the kitchen table and spent the afternoon putting it back together. So my grandmother was of the opinion that not only would a man be a threat, he would be an intrusion, wholly unnecessary.

The fact that my mother was moving so steadily toward middle age meant that my grandmother would soon have a grand companion, one more like herself. If my grandmother could've populated the world, all the people would've been women, and they all would've been just like her. And if she had been able to attach a rope to my mother and pull her through time, she would've happily greeted her somewhere on the other side of fifty. My mother, she probably thought, would be adequate compensation for her lost sister. But instead my mother was eyeing another man, and that meant she would want to remain youthful. She would no doubt visit the Elizabeth Arden counter to learn how to accentuate those cheekbones. She would buy ultra violet lipstick, a new panty girdle, satin pumps, and an Omar Kiam cocktail dress. The problem, though, was that my mother resisted any sort of tugging. She had the will sufficient to go her own way, which is what she did. When we got home that evening, she went straight for the telephone, took it with her into the coat closet, and shut the door. My grandmother sat and stared at the closet door, frowning. After my mother came back out, my grandmother asked, "When's he coming?"

My mother said, "Tomorrow night, if that's okay with everybody. If not, I'm sorry." Then she went to her room and left my grandmother and me alone in the living room. My grandmother jerked the radio on, turned the dial through every station, and jerked it off. Then she announced she was going to sleep, and suggested I do the same. I didn't. I sat up into the wee hours of the morning and finished *The Yearling*. When I finally went to bed, I saw that her light was still on, so I pushed open the door and was almost knocked down by the odor of Vicks VapoRub, which she always put in a noisy hot-water vaporizer and smeared underneath her nostrils when she sensed that air wasn't moving freely in and out of her system. She sat up in bed and asked me why I wasn't asleep. I told her I had finished the novel, and I wanted to report that something did indeed happen in it.

Before I could say anything else, she interrupted me. "I know," she said. "The deer dies."

I asked how she knew. She said, "I could see it coming. The problem was that not enough happened while she was getting there. Go to bed."

My mother woke up early and started organizing herself to get to town when the stores opened. She returned a few hours later with an astonishing Alice blue silk dress. We barely had dinner ready on time, unaccustomed as we were to preparing a full-course meal. My mother all but took over the kitchen, seeming with her new joy to be everywhere at once. My grandmother's only comment was, "You need a traffic cop in here. If you were cooking blind you could not have made a bigger mess." Her refusal to help didn't surprise me, and when she was called late in the afternoon to deliver the sixth baby of a very obnoxious Christian Scientist lady who had yet to pay her for the first five, she didn't grumble. She left quickly.

Mr. Baines arrived on time and with flowers and chocolate-covered cherries. If he had been any more charming, I doubt I would've trusted him. My job was to greet him and then entertain him in the living room, and then when he had had just enough time to wonder where in the world that handsome woman could be, my mother would enter. I chatted with Mr. Baines about my career plans, which I exaggerated so much that when I finished talking to him I was greatly enthused about all the opportunities in the field of medicine. He said a few things about his job, where he had gone to school, things like that. My mother must have been waiting to hear a lapse in our conversation. She walked into the room, and he stood to meet her. She held out a hand and said without speaking, "I'm what you have lived your whole life to get to. I'm why you were born. You are one lucky man."

95

He was shaken to the point that when he stood to greet her he had to press the tips of his fingers on the arm of his chair for balance. My mother asked him if he was being looked after, and once he had swallowed the lump in his throat, he said that he was indeed. Then he sat down, or rather his knees unlocked and down he went. My mother displayed herself on the sofa across the room from him so he could get a glorious, full-length vision of her, and from the way he squeezed the arm of the chair, it seemed almost more than he could bear. I think that had he known she was reading *To Have and Have Not* at the time and considered it anything but scandalous, he would've been too amazed to speak. And furthermore, if he had seen her race into a stranger's house, hike her dress up, and sit on a moaning husband's chest to hold him still while my grandmother worked on what they called a butcher-knife accident, he would've considered my mother more than he could handle, and he would've run from our house. If he had seen her confronting my school librarian over the decision to pull Sinclair Lewis novels off the shelves, and winning, he would've wondered whether he was up to the challenge. As it was, he could barely deal with her outward appearance, shimmering as she was in her Alice blue silk.

She said, "Mr. Baines, I thought I heard you say you went to college in Atlanta."

He cleared his throat and said, "Yes, I went to law school there, and then I lived there until a couple of years ago, when my wife and I divorced. I moved to Charlotte, then here."

I looked at my mother. She took the part about law school in admirably. I watched the great dial in her head rotate, passing things she wanted to ask, such as how much money did he make, was there family money involved, did he defend poor colored people for free or had he grown out of that, all questions of this nature. Instead, she cocked her head and looked at him and said nothing. He stared back. I thought that after a minute or so of looking at each other, one of them would've grown embarrassed enough to stop, but they didn't. I was the only one made uncomfortable by all this staring, so I got up and put dinner on the table. By the time they came to the dining room they had passed through the earliest, awkward stage of their love, and now they were asking questions of each other with the rapidity of a school spelling match. In a very short while they gathered all the basic information. By the time they sat down at the table, they seemed more than content, thrilled actually, to have discovered that they were just alike, and so they went back to gazing at each other. I considered saying I wasn't hungry, excusing myself to my room, but I wanted to watch this. And hear it. I wanted to hear my mother laugh the way she was meant to, and I wanted to see her blush, as she did repeatedly. There had never been a meal like this at our table. My mother's soul was fed as well as her body, and that sufficed to keep the two bound together, as they were supposed to be.

Mr. Baines stayed until nearly midnight, and had my grandmother been hiding in the bushes, waiting for his car to leave, she could not have timed her return any better. She came in as we were cleaning up the dishes. She was blood-spattered, and she was holding on to her right shoulder, which she tended to pull during forceps deliveries. Her left hip was also bothering her—another delivery injury she had received as a consequence of a woman's suddenly drawing back her knees, catching my grandmother underneath her armpits, and driving her across the room, where she landed on a child's wagon. My mother mixed a deep-heating compound and had my grandmother undress to her slip so she could massage it in. Nobody said anything about Mr. Baines. Instead, my grandmother filled that midnight hour with grousing about the self-righteous Christian Scientist husband who tripped and fell into the floor fan while his wife was in the final stage of labor. He refused my grandmother's help, so she told him, "Okay, bleed to death. That'd be the true blasphemy." After the baby was born, or rather, wrenched out of this woman, the husband consented to my grandmother's suggestion that she apply the resin of Saint-John's-wort to his cut. She told him the resin sprang from John the Baptist's blood when he was beheaded, which, according to legend, it did. Then she tended to the baby, ignoring the fact that the mother was ignoring the fact that a great deal of money was owed for those first five.

My grandmother thanked my mother for soothing her shoulder, and got up to pour a brandy. She stood there, smelling highly of peppermint camphor, threw back her brandy, and then wiped her mouth with the back of her hand, like a cowboy at the end of the bar. She put the glass in the sink and said, "I'm flabbergasted. Damn a Christian

Scientist." Then she headed off to bed. My mother couldn't stand it any longer, so she called after her, "Mother! Aren't you going to ask how dinner went?" Still walking down the hall, my grandmother shouted back, "No. I know how it went. When's he coming again?" My mother yelled, "Saturday!" just as my grandmother shut her door and limped across the room to her vaporizer. She must have hoped that by plugging it in she could drown out Christian Scientists, the neighbor's howling dogs, and Mr. Baines's tumultuous wee-hour dreams of my mother.

M<small>R. BAINES</small> was glory in my mother's life. He came to our house almost every night for dinner, always showing up in one of his beautiful suits, his straight white teeth gleaming, giddy as a forty-year-old man could be without appearing drunk, retarded, or foolish. After dinner he would sit on the sofa with his arm around my mother's shoulders and talk about places he wanted to take her. He compiled such a long list that after a while I worried that the plans would never materialize. My grandmother noticed this as well, and asked my mother several times, "Well, where'd he take you tonight?" They were never grand places, and his attitude was not that of a self-satisfied traveler who wanted to impress this homebound woman with how much he'd seen of the world. He wanted to take her to Middleton Plantation in Charleston to show her the ancient live oak tree because she'd look so pretty standing next to it in a picture. He wanted to take her to Cypress Gardens because she'd look radiant in the light. He wanted to take her to the Homestead resort because she deserved to be pampered.

The first place they went together was Charlotte. Mr. Baines closed up his family's home there and brought his elderly mother back to Raleigh to live with him. She suffered from a form of dementia that would later be called Alzheimer's. She brought all her ferns with her on the train. They had lined her porch in Charlotte. My mother told us how she arranged the ferns around her feet, in her lap, in my mother's lap, stroked them as if they were lapdogs, and repeated all the way to Raleigh, "Maidenhair fern, very pretty. Lady fern, very pretty. Angel's hair, very pretty. Boston fern, also very pretty." My mother helped settle Mrs. Baines into her bedroom, and she wrapped the planters in green tissue and tied large red bows around them, winning the old woman's heart, as she suspected she would.

Although my grandmother was not yet too fond of Mr. Baines, she stepped in to help with his mother. She wanted to make sure the woman's needs were well met. She called all the hospitals in the county and located a private duty nurse for her. She interviewed several women before finally hiring one who did not appear to be lying when she said she would not allow Mrs. Baines to wander out into traffic or sit around in soiled underthings while she lazed off in front of the radio.

If Mr. Baines had never taken my mother anywhere but Charlotte, she would've been content to sit by him three hours a night in that one spot, with my grandmother sitting across from them, pretending to read. When they did leave the house, it was on foot. They'd take our old railroad lantern and walk the trail by Crabtree Creek for hours. My grandmother would decide when it was past time for them to be home, and would start watching the back door, saying things like, "I hate to think what they could be doing out there. Those woods are owned by the city. If they got caught doing something, the newspaper would have a big time with the story. They're old enough to do it at home. That's where they should do it." Several times I caught my mother coming back in and whispered for her to check her clothing, particularly her skirts, which would be twisted around her hips. Mr. Baines always stopped and combed his hair and straightened his tie in the cloudy mirror that hung over the utility sink.

One evening, deep into that exceptionally cold January of 1940, they ignored my grandmother's frostbite warnings and went out anyway. I helped bundle them up as if they were my children, and sent them out with the lantern, making them promise as I turned up the wick that they wouldn't be gone for too long. I fell asleep listening for the door to creak. After midnight, I woke up feeling a coldness next to me, not a sharp chill, but a spready, cloudlike sensation of the sort one would notice with a ghost beside the bed. It was my mother, stooped over with her face inches from mine. She looked so tender in the dim light. She asked if she could sleep with me and borrow my heat. I said she could, and she crawled over me to get to the other side of the bed, saying as she nestled underneath the covers, "I have never felt such wind." The night had been still, and so I asked her where the wind had come from. She explained that during the walk she had mentioned her unfulfilled desire to ice skate, and how the fear of broken bones had been the only thing that ever stopped her. Mr. Baines then walked her back to the house, crept inside and got a dining room chair, put it in the trunk of his car, and drove her to Lassiter Mill Pond. He pushed her about on the frozen pond while she sat in the chair, head back and legs out, as if she were riding a swing. As my mother lay there with her dress on and her stockings, I could feel the cold night air still about her. She turned on her side with her back to me. She was asleep before I could take all the pins out of her hair, warm now, melting in love.

In the next months, Mr. Baines took her everywhere he said he would. She stayed in a swivet, packing and unpacking, rushing film to the drugstore, pasting snapshots in a new album. She would write underneath them in white ink, her head down almost touching the page, concentrating on neatness and style as if she were copying penmanship lessons. It seemed that every other page had a snapshot captioned: "Sophia having the time of her life."

She became so attached to him that after he had spent a day with her, particularly a Sunday, she would cry when he left. As his car disappeared down the highway, she would press her cheek to the windowpane and whimper like a lonesome pet. She generally had terrible monthlies, and during especially rough ones her reaction to his leaving was highly dramatic. She would lie across her bed and sob, threatening to present herself at the door of the state asylum. She would say, "Maybe I need to be locked up. I don't feel so good." When she was cried out, she would wash her face, dose herself up with evening primrose oil and False Unicorn, and pretend to pay attention to the radio, and after enough hours had passed for her to have forgiven him for leaving, she would start to smile again. And after more time had gone by, she would be reeling in love, showing me whatever trinket he had most recently brought her, things like marcasite earrings, pearl hatpins, and leather-bound editions of her favorite books.

But if my grandmother was around, she'd force herself to tolerate his departure, no matter how furiously her hormones were warring inside her. If my grandmother had seen such an excess of emotion, she would've warned her of an even sadder day to come, the day Mr. Baines would drive off and keep on driving. Then would come the fight. Charles Nutter would be flagged about, as well as my father and his yellow wedding shoes, his girlfriends, and if things really escalated, my mother would ask her mother why, exactly, her own husband had left. And so, if it took my mother's biting herself to hide these departure miseries from my grandmother, she would do it. The alternative bruised her spirit, as well as my grandmother's, and mine.

I realized fairly early into my mother's courtship that in order to live in the same house with these two women, I would need to decide whom I would defend over what issue and when. Usually I chose my grandmother, as I believed she possessed the wisdom of the ages, and when I saw my mother buck and kick against her authority, I would gently say, "Don't you think Grandmother's probably been through this, and so she might sort of know what to do?" If my mother responded to me at all, it was to say something like, "She's been through twenty more years than I have. That's it."

In a very bold mood, my mother announced she was not going out on any more house calls that might cause her to miss a date with Mr. Baines. My grandmother went haywire-flooey. She shouted, "Suppose Sophia Snow had had a date when you were born? We'd both be in the ground!" My mother backed down, and out the three of us would go whenever a call came. My mother would tie tourniquets, set broken fingers, wrap sprained ankles, build bronchitis tents, doing everything perfectly, but with one eye on the clock. She almost always managed to make it home on time, even though more than once she met Mr. Baines at the door with dried blood still underneath her fingernails and plaster of Paris flecking the soft hair around her face.

My grandmother made her miss only one date, but at least I was able to leave the patient's house and speed through half the county to stop Mr. Baines just as he was turning out onto the highway, looking confused and forlorn, driving slumped over the wheel, as if he had been shot in the back. I took him to our house and sat inside with him until my mother and grandmother came home, or rather, until my grandmother came in and told Mr. Baines to go lift my mother out of the backseat of their ride's car. He looked so alarmed that I regretted having avoided telling him what had happened to my mother on the house call.

She had fainted and awakened vomiting at the home of

an old man known as the Hermit Willoughby, and as she was to say later, "Yes, I did it, and with good reason." My grandmother had been called to his house early that afternoon, and she insisted that both my mother and I go with her, as she didn't know what she'd find when she got there. The Hermit Willoughby had lived alone since the death of his mother twenty years before, subsisting on handouts that Sunday-school classes left by his door and on whatever he could shoot or trap or cause to grow in the swampy wetlands around his cabin. The news that he needed medical help came to us by way of a rural relay of sorts that involved no fewer than three tenant farmers, a housewife or two, the postman, and a stranger who was pumping gas at a store. He showed up at our door and said, "I was asked to come here to tell you that the hermit has cut his throat." My grandmother knew whom he meant. She rounded us up and we left hurriedly, my mother huffing because she was given no time either to call Mr. Baines or to leave him a note.

My automatic reaction upon entering the man's house was to put my hand to my mouth and pinch my nostrils with my fingers. The place called to mind Miss Havisham's scrambled and filthy dining room in *Great Expectations,* only a thousand times worse. My mother's reaction was to stick by the door, which she kept propped open with one foot to give herself some fresh air. What did my grandmother do? She plowed forward, edging kittens and baby rabbits and chewed ears of corn out of her path, until she reached the Hermit Willoughby. He was sitting at a rough wooden table with his head in his hands. She said, "You smell like Satan.

They're saying you cut your throat." And then, looking about the cabin, she added, "So why didn't you?" He lifted his head, and when he did I saw why we were there. His throat was covered by a massive boil that seemed to have crawled up from his chest through the neck of his greasy undershirt, and if this thing had had a voice, it would've screamed its rage and vengeance. He didn't say anything to my grandmother. He just blinked at her, very slowly, like a turtle. On the table beside him lay an open pocketknife, which my grandmother picked up and shook at him, saying, "Did you use this? Did you go after that boil with this?" He blinked again.

My grandmother shouted, "Come on, you two! Let's start on him!" My mother and I dragged ourselves over to her. I resigned myself to doing anything but touching his neck. My mother glanced around the kitchen, sighed, and said, "Well, I guess rubber gloves are out of the question." I pumped water at the sink, and my grandmother washed her hands and arms. Then I laid her sterile cloth on the table and displayed the instruments I knew she would need. As she circled the man's chair, contemplating exactly how to proceed, she asked him to tell her how he had gotten his neck into this hideous condition.

He told her he had started going after the boil the day before, and could not stop, driven as he was by that lurid curiosity and involuntary compulsion that makes some people incapable of leaving their bodies alone. He had used the fish-scaling, can-opening, pedicuring pocketknife that now lay beside him, and he had resorted to this only after a week's worth of magical cures had failed him. My grand-mother asked if he had learned the cures from his parents. He said he had.

According to local legend, his mother had been a true witch and his father a warlock. In order to find all the charms for his incantations, he had left his house for the first time in twenty years, and had gotten as far as the crossroads when he discovered that the world had changed so much that he didn't know which road to choose. He remembered the old signposts—the stone well, the big stump, the owl tree—but now all these things were gone. So he stood there in the middle of the crossroads, with this boil throbbing a purple spasm on his throat, scaring the smittens out of women and children as he flagged down cars and asked after his charms: "Where is a faithful wife? Where is a blind dog? Where is a black cat, and does it belong to an old hag? Where is a white nigger with pink rabbit eyes?" He collected everything. It took him all day. He sponged his boil with the urine of the faithful wife. He caused a blind dog to lick his neck by lathering the spot with hog grease. He held the black cat's tail and made the sign of the cross over the boil. He used the dirty handkerchief of an accommodating albino to tie a slice of raw onion around his neck. None of these things worked. When he felt worse, and when the red streak started its course toward his heart, he put a toad under a pot and walked around it three times. He swallowed lead shot to absorb the poison. He pricked the boil with a gooseberry thorn until his blood ran black to red, and then he tossed the thorn over his left shoulder. None of these things worked

either. When he developed a spiking fever, he walked back
down to the crossroads and sent for my grandmother, whom
he had met right before his mother died, when she appeared
at the door to ask permission to take herb cuttings from her
yard. Upon looking at his mother, my grandmother diag-
nosed her with Bell's palsy, a condition the woman attributed to the evil eye someone had cast upon her. My
grandmother held forth on neurological disorders, making
such an impression on the son that he remembered her for
years as somebody who sounded like she knew what she was
talking about. That was almost exactly what he told my
grandmother: "I thought you might know what to do about
me. Ma being dead and all." She assured him that she did.
He was near tears as he continued: "I did not care to die.
I like being by myself too much. I'm not ready to go be
around everybody that's ever died. That's a lot of people."

My grandmother agreed that it was indeed, and then she
told my mother to stand ready by his neck with a basin. She
said, "Don't be particular. Just grab anything you can find
that'll hold all this matter. It doesn't have to be clean. This
stuff certainly isn't." My mother poked around the kitchen
counter and finally produced a ceramic bowl that looked as
if it hadn't been washed in years. She stood beside my
grandmother, holding the bowl out as far from her body as
she could. She was staring at the man's neck sideways. She
looked woozy. My job was to hand over instruments, starting first with a benzocaine swab, which my grandmother
took from me and held before the hermit's yellow eyes,
saying, "You see this? This won't hurt. Everything else will,

but this won't." She swabbed his neck, humming as she did. Then she stood behind his chair and said, "Now lean back. Ease your neck."

She put both her hands on his head as if it were a cabbage she was about to wash and cut up for slaw, and after much turning it this way and that, she rested it on her stomach. She seemed satisfied that it was settled in at the best angle. I asked whether she was ready to proceed, and she nodded and reached her hand flat out to me. And then, with the scalpel in her hand and so far up in the air, she looked as if she could easily and without a dash of emotion cut his throat from ear to ear. Before she brought her hand down she told him not to yell, or it would make her nervous. She said, "My hand will slip and you will surely die." Then she told my mother to get ready. She made two rapid crossed incisions oh so close to his jugular, and then shouted, "God-dammit, Sophia! Where's the basin?" It was clattering on the floor, where my mother had just dropped.

I didn't know what to do, and I looked for my grand-mother to tell me. She told me to pick up the basin, catch the drainage, and swab the wound so she could have a clearer view of things. "Let's hurry this along," she said. "Just straddle Sophia while we finish." So I stood with one foot on either side of my mother's chest and swallowed back what I felt to be a gallon of saliva while I cleaned the hermit's wound with iodine and hydrogen peroxide. My grand-mother then began hurriedly coating his neck with ichtham-mol salve, glancing down at my mother every few seconds, getting more salve in his hair than on the wound. She was very distracted. It was the first time I had seen her rush through a routine procedure. I offered to take over. She nodded and told the man to sit still while she tended to my mother, cold as death as she was, still unconscious among pet rabbit droppings, dog hair, and the other decayed or decaying matter of a hermit's life. She awakened when my grandmother passed ammonia under her nostrils, and then she turned her head to the side and vomited. When she was through, she looked up at me and said, "Go tell Richard I'm dead. I can't go to the movies." Once again, I looked to my grandmother for instruction. She said, "Go ahead. Drive home and tell him she'll be late. I'll drag her home before long. I'll go to the crossroads and flag a ride."

So that would account for why Mr. Baines blanched when he opened the car door and saw my mother in a heap on the backseat. The man who had given them the ride looked as though he expected to be paid, and Mr. Baines opened his wallet and gave the man more money than he probably made in three months. Mr. Baines carried my mother inside, slung across his shoulder as if he were taking her off a battlefield, and in a way I guess he was. When he laid her across her bed, she started to whimper that she never wanted to go through that again. When he asked how she had gotten in this shape, my grandmother said, "Sophia's always been weak about running infection. Plus she didn't eat breakfast this morning." Then she excused herself to the kitchen, saying, "I think I'm going to fix a little glass of whiskey. I think that would be in order." I heard ice hit the glass, and then I heard her shout out loud, "Mr. Baines!

Would you care to take a drink? Sophia's already made you too late for the movies. Might as well have one." My mother and I were shocked at this miraculous offer. She motioned for Mr. Baines to go on to the kitchen, saying groggily, "My mother has lost touch with her reason. Take advantage of it." He left the room, and as I helped my mother out of her dress and into a sandalwood-flake bath, we heard more miracles, my grandmother laughing with him, telling funny stories about delivering backwoods babies.

My mother and I never asked my grandmother why she so suddenly changed her attitude about Mr. Baines. If we had asked her, either she would've told us it was none of our business—a response we could've tolerated because we always had—or she would've started ignoring him again out of some childlike mixture of defiance and embarrassment over having flashed a light into such a rarely seen corner of herself. We didn't want this to happen. Days later, when my mother's curiosity had eaten a nearly visible place in her, I volunteered an answer. I told her she had looked dead there on the floor, as dead as a person could appear and still be breathing. Her face was pale from having the blood rush downward so quickly. Her lips were blue. It would've been disturbing for any mother to see her child crumpled on the floor like that, but in this case it was much worse, because my grandmother was so familiar with death, and there it seemed to lie by her feet. And while I hesitate to romanticize the event by saying that my grandmother realized how suddenly she could lose her daughter, and thus made some sort of silent promise to try to let her have the life she wanted, I'm convinced this is what happened.

THE DAY of my senior dance in March 1940, my mother and grandmother received a large brown envelope from the school principal. He was concerned that I had not yet applied for college, and so he had taken it upon himself to acquire brochures from the schools he believed most suitable for me. His list was impressive: Smith, Wellesley, Vassar, Radcliffe, Bennington, Bryn Mawr, and Goucher. When they showed me the letter, I was somewhat discomforted to see how excited he was over the idea that I would be the first woman in recent years to graduate from Coopers High School and go on to something more challenging than Hardbarger's Secretarial College. It was as if he were taking personal responsibility for my grades and what he called my "modesty, excellent goodwill, and temperate disposition." I didn't sound very interesting, nothing like my grandmother. I was worried that she would heap ridicule on the letter and shout things like,

"Good God, Margaret! You sound like Pollyanna!" But she did not. She read the letter through several times, smiling broadly. My mother asked me which of these schools I wanted to attend.

I said, "I have absolutely no idea. If I had to make the decision today, I think I'd just stay at home."

My mother said, "Don't be silly. You can't stay at home."

My grandmother didn't say anything to me. She just sat there, studying my face.

I meant what I said. I had lain awake many nights and thought about this, how all the best schools were far from home. It wasn't that I imagined myself alone on a campus where nobody was familiar to me except characters in books I had already read. That vision didn't concern me. But when I saw myself peeking through the window of my mother's house, my grandmother and her without me, getting ready to go out on a house call or walking back in tired and bloodstained, I could barely breathe. The only way I could make the anxiety abate was to remind myself that I didn't have to go anywhere. I could get all the education I needed or wanted, for the time being, at home.

In our house, the point of reading and learning was neither to impress outsiders nor to get a job or a husband, nothing like that. It had nothing to do with anybody but the three of us. When a good book was in the house, the place fairly vibrated. We trained ourselves to be exceptionally fast readers so a book could be traded around before the nagging and tugging became intolerable. I remember particularly, when *The Grapes of Wrath* was new, how my mother and grandmother felt I wasn't reading it quickly enough, how they asked me every half-hour or so how far along I was. When I suggested we take an afternoon-and-evening vacation and read it together, they sat down on the sofa and patted the spot between them, as if I were a puppy they were coaxing to jump up. We took turns holding the book, turning pages, and the only times we got up in twelve hours were to turn on a light and go to the bathroom.

We shared a curiosity about the world that couldn't be satisfied in any other way. Maybe my grandmother approached this sort of satisfaction with her passion for medicine, but still she would sit for hours and contemplate the disappearance of that opening narrator in *Madame Bovary* with the same intensity with which she would line up a patient's symptoms and then labor over a diagnosis. Hardy was her favorite novelist, and she knew his work as well as she knew the signs of cirrhosis and diabetes. She and my mother could fight like mad about any issue of the day except what a toad Madame Bovary was. They went over and over her life, talking about her as if she were real. One morning they fought over some trifling matter, and then pouted all day until my grandmother looked up from a novel and said, "Sophia! This character reminds me of Madame Bovary. Did you think she had that nasty death coming to her? Was she that bad a strumpet? Tell me. I'm interested." My mother sat down by her and explained how she thought Madame Bovary deserved that and more, and then they spread on into *Jude the Obscure* and *Far from the Madding Crowd*. It was as if they had completely forgotten that three hours before, they had called each other the vilest sorts of names, names as low-down as those they had just chosen for Madame Bovary.

With regard to the colleges, my mother wouldn't let me stop with "I have absolutely no idea." I tried to pacify her by going on to say that I'd think about all this later, but when I got up to go to my room, she was right behind me. I asked if she planned to hang about me like Grant hung about Richmond, and after laughing a second, she closed the door to my room and said very sternly, "You need to be serious. This is your future."

It would've been impossible to tell her that I much preferred to talk with my grandmother about my future. As smart as my mother was, I was afraid to trust her. I couldn't forget how she had married the type of man who would make a joke of his wedding day and all the days after. Even if my father had been alive, he wouldn't have been moved by the principal's letter. He wouldn't have been proud or gratified, even secretly, that he had the sort of daughter who could compete at a fine college. He would've been oblivious to it. He wouldn't have *gotten* it. And so, while my mother sat on the edge of my bed, waiting for me to tell her my wishes and desires, to purge for her, the woman I really wanted to talk to was in the kitchen pressing pills, wondering whether my mother would go to sleep early so she and I could get a head start on our inevitable discussion.

By the time my mother did go to bed, I was so weary from having fended her off all day that I almost told my grandmother we'd have to get up early in the morning to do this.

But I couldn't. When she tapped on my door and stepped into the room, I could tell that she had everything figured out. She knew exactly what I was to do with myself, and I suspected that it did not include long, bitter winters in Vermont or Massachusetts.

She pulled out my desk chair, sat down hard the way she always did, and said, "Well, what do you think of all this?"

I said, "You know I don't want to leave home."

She asked me why, even though she knew why. She was checking behind me to see how far I had come in my life, what I had learned along the way.

Before she had come into the room, I had rehearsed the things I would say. I would tell her about lying in bed, seeing myself peeking in the house, seeing my mother and her going about their business without me. I would tell her about how my panic had left me when I decided that I wouldn't leave home. But I wasn't able to say any of this. All I could do was sit up in my bed and toy with the satin edge of my blanket and wonder what she would do if I let loose and cried as hard as I needed to.

She reached into her pocket and took out a postcard. She told me it was a note Charles Nutter had once sent her from medical school, and then she said, "You remind me of him. Listen."

September 6, 1917

Dear Miss Charlie Kate,
    I don't know how I'll ever thank you enough for

119

making this possible. This is such an extraordinary place. You were right. What a fine thing it is—finally—not to be the only one, but one of many.

Sincerely,
Charles Nutter

My grandmother slipped the postcard back into her pocket and said, "If you'll go to college, you'll say that, too. You'll be exposed to a great many girls like yourself."

I told her I had thought about this, but I still didn't want to leave home.

She said, "Well then, nobody's going to force you to go anywhere, not now. You should eventually. Next year or the next. You know that. I'm afraid that if you go somewhere you don't want to go, you'll be miserable and you won't learn a drop. Your mother's stubborn nature will surely blossom in you and take over." And then she smiled and said, "And you'd be wasting my money."

By now I was crying in great heaving sobs. I asked her what I would say to my mother. She told me not to worry about her. She would take care of that.

The next day I saw and heard the first consequence of my grandmother's taking care of things. She and my mother walked in the house from a routine call they had gone out on while I was in school. My mother slid her purse across the kitchen counter and said, "Well! I understand you and your grandmother are in cahoots now for certain!"

I explained that we had decided that I would stay home for a while, not forever. I would go to school in a year or so.

And then I lied and said that I had exhausted myself in high school and I needed and deserved a break.

My mother drew herself up in the manner in which Southern women draw themselves up, and said, "That's just fine! While you're here sitting at the feet of Dr. Birch, all the other girls your age are going to snatch up all the decent young men and leave you the dregs."

I told her I didn't care. This made her as mad as I'd ever seen her. She screamed, "You'd better care!"

My grandmother told her to hush and go to bed with some laudanum, and then she jerked on the faucet to wash her hands, muttering something about my mother's being the expert on dregs, philanderers, and things of that nature. They began trading insults, and they stopped only when I asked them please not to kill each other while I was at the dance. My mother looked at the clock and asked me why I was leaving for a dance at four in the afternoon. I reminded her that I was in charge of the decorations.

She shouted, "See what I mean?"

Yes, I knew. I didn't have a date or a new party dress. I would spend the evening patrolling the parking lot, asking hoodlums from the vocational school to move along, and they would move along, too, because I would ask them in such a firm yet friendly way. They wouldn't hoot at me or wink or say anything remotely lascivious because I would appear to be so much older, sort of like somebody's mother. Why didn't I have a date? The one boy who would've asked me transferred to Lawrenceville Academy. That left fifty or so boys who would never have asked me to a dance, but who regularly asked me to correct their term papers, show them how to use the library card catalogue, intercede in disputes with their girlfriends, and forge absentee excuses from their parents in my mature and thoroughly convincing handwriting. None of these boys ever looked up at me, as I explained for the tenth time that Twain was cross-referenced with Clemens, and said, "It's you. You're the one." No, if they looked into my eyes and said anything, it was, "Boy, Margaret, how'd you learn all this stuff?"

The caption underneath my senior-year yearbook photograph read "Most Admired," "Smartest Girl," and "Most Likely to Succeed." Underneath that ran the long list of my honors and extracurricular activities. I am smiling, but just slightly, and my eyes look tired. I had stayed up all the previous night working on an essay on Edith Wharton, which my teacher secretly entered in a literary contest. It won first place: ten dollars and an invitation to have tea with a local writer named Inglis Fletcher. I declined the latter, making up some sort of excuse, but really I didn't go because of my grandmother's attitude toward her writing, which she considered amateurish and romantic, unremarkable in any way. She said, "Now, if you could meet James Thurber, that'd be worth doing. Don't you know *he* could hold forth?"

I worked terribly hard in school. During study hall I worked in the principal's office. I also helped out in the nurse's office, but not at a regularly scheduled time. She would call me over the intercom when she needed me, and when I got to her office, she would point to a student and say, "Him. I don't know what to do about him." Although I felt confident diagnosing sinusitis, bronchitis, and other sorts of seasonal ills, the degree to which the nurse trusted me to assess a student's condition made me so uneasy that I sometimes telephoned my grandmother and described symptoms. In fact, I did this so much during polio and influenza outbreaks that my grandmother asked to sit in on my honors English class as a sort of payment. We were studying the history of the American novel, a subject she knew well. I was afraid the teacher would err, and when she did, my grandmother raised her hand and said, "Pardon me, but *The Last of the Mohicans* came fifteen years before *The Deerslayer,* not that you'd want to read either one of them." The teacher attributed her mistake to transposed dates in her notes, and spent the rest of the period on *The Scarlet Letter,* which was her specialty. She would make pronouncements on plot and theme and then look straight at my grandmother, daring her to disagree. She didn't, but only because her mind had drifted. Later, when I asked her why she had appeared so preoccupied, she told me she had been roaming the streets of Boston. "I was thinking what a hellish time that must've been to live in," she said. "No plumbing, running sewage, cholera, botulism, dysentery. All these sorts of things. I would've been worked to a frazzle."

I was considered such a part of the school staff that I was given a pass key. When the principal gave it to me, he didn't lecture me about what a big responsibility it was, how I was being entrusted with record players, sports equipment, and books with the answers in the back. He just gave it to me and said it would come in handy when I needed to set the gym up for dances or work late on county attendance records. He told me to toss the key back in his desk drawer when I graduated.

That's how I unlocked the school late that afternoon and went through the storage closets and pulled out tape and staplers and crepe paper to use in decorating the gym. When I had done all I could do alone, I sat on a bleacher and waited for the rest of my committee. I waited and waited, and just about when I was giving up on having any sort of help, I heard a voice in the lobby saying, "Sophia! This is a perfectly fine thing to do on a date. Don't you think, Richard?" I looked at the door, and in came my grandmother and mother and Mr. Baines. My grandmother walked across the gym floor talking loudly. "They couldn't think of what to do. They've seen all the movies, and they're sick of eating out. I suggested we all come to your party." She was dressed in her mourning garb, which in its own odd way was the fanciest thing she had, especially when she decorated her bosom with the elaborate cat's-eye brooch Mr. Baines had surprised her with on her birthday. He had it designed according to her descriptions of one her aunt had worn. My mother was wearing a slim-fitting burgundy velvet dress, very simple and very *chic*—a word which, for all our learning, my grandmother, my mother, and I never pronounced correctly.

By the time the rest of my committee arrived, we had the gym almost finished, and Mr. Baines, my mother, and my grandmother continued to help on into the evening. Mr.

Baines volunteered to patrol the parking lot in between dances with my mother. My grandmother retaped sagging crepe paper to the walls in between discussions with the English teacher she had chastised. And then later, both she and my mother helped me calm a crying girl I knew only by her reputation for cheating who had started her monthly and spotted up her dress and would not come out of the bathroom. My grandmother used the steak knife she always hid in her purse to break into the jammed sanitary supply machine and get the girl what she needed, and my mother traded dresses with her and spent the rest of the evening in a homemade affair she otherwise would not have been buried in. My mother wore her black linen coat over the girl's dress to hide not only the stain but the crooked topstitching on the sagging bodice as well. When the girl came out of the bathroom and found her date, he acted as if he hadn't come with her, as if he didn't know her at all. She found the three of us and started bawling again like a madwoman. My grandmother backed this boy up in a narrow space between two sets of bleachers and shouted directly into his face. I went to check on her and was flabbergasted to look down at their feet and see that she held one of her shoes from the last century right down on top of one of his wingtips. I do not know what all she said to him, but the boy sought out his date and spent the rest of the evening seemingly happy to be with her.

A few months later I graduated first in my class. Writing my valedictory address was somewhat of a challenge, because I felt I couldn't talk about embracing the future when

I was so committed to keeping my life just the way it was. I ended up quoting heavily from *The Way of All Flesh,* which was not at all pertinent but was fresh in my mind, as I had just finished reading it. The speech went as well as it could have, if you consider that the audience was hot and squirmy, trying to keep cool using the cardboard fans somebody from a funeral home had handed out at the door. My grand-mother went completely out of herself to stand and clap when the superintendent introduced me and then an-nounced that I had won a countywide award given each year in the memory of the valedictorian of 1920, who, unlike me, exercised her potential immediately upon graduation and attended Wellesley College, where she contracted German measles and died in her first semester. After a few seconds of looking up at my grandmother and then all around to realize she was the only person up on her feet, Mr. Baines and my mother also stood. The other people didn't know exactly what to do. Some stood. Some halfway stood and applauded sort of hunched over. They weren't sure what the rules were. My grandmother didn't care what they were. She felt moved to rise, so that's what she did. And then she sat back down with my mother and Mr. Baines in the first row of the parents' section, nodding whenever she heard a line she had given me the night before. I remember the closing lines she gave me: "You will remember 1940 as the year before your life changed. For many of you, this may be your last good year for a long time, unless you're lucky enough to have flat feet."

INDEED, 1940 would be the last normal year for all of us. Everybody I knew spent the next year wondering when Mr. Roosevelt would do what we knew he was dying to do. Our house was so full of worry over what seemed to be ahead. My grandmother would listen to the radio and make horrible predictions. Sometimes I felt as if I were looking out at a pink sky and sensing the air pressure drop, the way it does before a tornado. That's what kept me from enrolling in college for the fall term of 1941, that feeling of waiting for something terrible to happen, not wanting to leave the house and get caught in what the sky, and my grandmother, told me was coming. Maybe it was nothing more than another excuse, but what an excellent one. Now I could wait out a war. I wouldn't have to leave home until the millions of people who my grandmother said would die had died.

I gained weight those two years, leading a contemplative

life on our sofa, reading things like Sophocles, Euripides, Homer, and Aeschylus, and listening to the war news on the radio and plotting troop movements on a large *National Geographic* map my mother had pinned to the living room wall. Also, she, my grandmother, and I became addicted to quiz programs, particularly *Dr. I.Q.* The two of them talked back to the show's host as if he could hear them, as if they expected him to respond. Wanting him to be rougher on contestants who didn't know answers, they yelled things like, "Don't give the man another chance! He's a *doofus*! Anybody who doesn't know who won at Bull Run is a *doofus*!" Mr. Baines, being such a kind and gentle person, would try to defend the host, but they would run over him. Any answers they didn't know, and there were few, they would dismiss as superfluous detail. My grandmother was all but unbeatable on questions pertaining to history, geography, medicine, and literature. My mother also excelled at questions about literature, but her main strengths were in the areas of popular music, movies, sentimental poetry, true crime, famous murders, how much Mr. Roosevelt weighed, how he ate only scrambled eggs on election nights, when his little dog Fala's birthday was.

Books and troop movements and the radio filled the time we had been spending on house calls. They were becoming more and more infrequent, for several reasons: health care at the county clinics improved, particularly with the broader use of sulfa drugs; more people were able to afford cars to take them there; and more muddy paths into the backwoods were blacktopped. My grandmother went for almost a year with no major case. This caused her to snipe at my mother more than usual, and this, in turn, raised my mother's level of backchat.

I remember how relieved my mother and I were when my grandmother's lawyer called upon her to offer a second opinion at a commitment hearing. The son of one of his clients suffered from what would later be known as Tourette's syndrome. The lawyer thought the boy should not be committed, but he couldn't tell his client this, since he wanted to keep the family's very considerable business. So he asked that my grandmother examine the boy and testify the following week, knowing, as he did, that the judge scheduled to preside at the hearing was an old friend of hers. This judge remarked to me once that he found her, of all things, charming. They had served together on the War Orphan Board as well as the State Committee on Inter-racial Cooperation. Although my grandmother could offer no official credentials, the judge was inclined to agree with anything she had to say. I went with her to the family's home to examine the boy. He stood in the center of the living room and did jumping jacks and cursed violently and could not be coaxed into submission. My grandmother sat and watched him, saying nothing. On the way home all she told me was that the boy needed to be seen by a specialist, and although she pitied his parents, she did not plan to recommend commitment.

The following week at the hearing, the boy was even wilder than he had been at his home. His father wept when he described how caring for him had become such a strain, how his other children had been ignored, and so forth. When my grandmother was asked to speak, she told the judge what she had told me, and she went on to prophesy that the boy would die a lonely, ignoble death in the asylum. She recommended, instead, that he be evaluated for treatment at the Menninger Clinic in Topeka. A doctor there had written several articles on this sort of neurological disorder. She had called the medical school at Chapel Hill and gotten this information. But counterbalancing her arguments was the boy himself, shouting, raging. The judge favored commitment, and before he announced his decision, he apologized to my grandmother and thanked her for her concern. The boy was taken to Dorothea Dix asylum and put on one of those crowded wards that were organized not by illness but by the patient's county of birth. A week later, he broke into the janitor's closet and ate drain crystals. My grandmother could not be consoled.

My mother insisted that my grandmother and I do Red Cross work with her, saying our mental health would deteriorate with so much time spent inside the house. We went with her a few times and helped pack boxes that were sent to Allied POWs. My mother read the very detailed list of instructions from the War Department. The contents of the boxes had to be packed a certain way. There could be no mistakes. I remember that the shaving soap, the cigarettes, and Hershey bars had to be upright, since deviations could be interpreted as codes. If the enemy found anything amiss with even one box, they would refuse the entire shipment or torture a soldier, whichever they pleased. My grandmother drove the other women at her table mad by checking and rechecking her boxes, repeating the contents aloud each time. One woman finally spoke up. She asked if my grandmother would please not repeat things so loudly. She was confusing the other workers. My grandmother said, "That is not my responsibility." Then she started again: "Zippo, upper right corner. Hershey bar, right side up, bottom right-hand corner. Two handkerchiefs, folded, rectangular, over the cigarettes, also right side up."

After my first day of packing these boxes, my nerves were shattered. I woke up screaming from a sweaty nightmare vision of some GI who looked like General Wainwright starving in a dark hole in the ground all because I had inserted a Hershey bar upside down in his package. It distressed me so greatly that I went into my mother's room and asked to be given the keys to the Red Cross storage building. I meant to check all the boxes. She talked me out of this by reminding me of all the ways and times I had been conscientious, and then she brewed me a calming tea of lemon balm and evening primrose and put me back to bed. The next time I went with her to the Red Cross and packed the boxes, I took each one I packed to her table and let her check behind me. She was very patient. She'd touch each item and say I'd placed it exactly right, her voice at the same calm level it had been at when I was a child bringing her my spelling homework to check.

For one three- or four-month stretch, about the only times I left the house were to go to the movies or the Red Cross with my mother and grandmother. I was finding that the less I left home, the easier it was to stay there. I knew how Thoreau felt in his little cabin, not to mention the Hermit Willoughby. And then my mother came up with another plan to get me out into the world. She began hounding me to go on blind dates with young men from Mr. Baines's office. I finally consented to going along on a double date with her and Mr. Baines, mainly because she wouldn't leave me alone, and partially because both she and Mr. Baines talked incessantly about how smart the young man was. I asked her where he had gone to college, and she lowered her voice what seemed like three octaves, touched my hand, and said, "Yale." Then she pulled her head back, pursed her lips, and waited for me to say something like, "Well, sign me up!" My grandmother walked in as my mother was dragging out "Yale" in her sonorous two-syllable drawl. She asked what was wrong with him: What was the catch? Why wasn't he fighting?

My mother snapped, "I've already asked. He has a punctured eardrum."

My grandmother said, "That's just what you need, Margaret, a man with a real excuse not to listen to you."

They spent the next ten minutes arguing about this remark, and when Mr. Baines arrived for dinner that evening, my mother met him at the door. I could hear her out on the porch, whispering to him as he straightened his tie in the utility mirror. "Can you believe her? Yale, for goodness' sakes. Can you believe her? She'll turn into one of these women like Gertrude Stein. Gertrude Stein and my mother." The problem was that she felt that in rejecting the offer, I was also rejecting her, or a piece of her, and the only way to persuade her to believe otherwise would've been to date the young man immediately and marry him the next morning.

His name escapes me, plowed under, I suppose, by the mind's ability to dismantle and hide pieces of unsavory experiences. But I do remember that the dinner was in the dining room of the Andrew Johnson Hotel and the harpist was too close to the table. My date was certainly intelligent enough, but in a grating, pompous sort of way. I remember his saying that he didn't believe in the novel as a form of literature, especially as the form was practiced by Faulkner. That's how he put it: "I don't believe his novels qualify as literature." He took particular issue with *The Hamlet,* quoting catchphrases from reviews he was sure I hadn't read, such as those by Clifton Fadiman and other critics who had missed the point of the novel. In fact, I had read Mr. Fadiman's derogatory review in *The New Yorker* while waiting for my grandmother to examine her string of patients at City News and Candy. I knew that if it disturbed me, it would cause my grandmother to have a stroke of paralysis, so I quickly hid all the *New Yorker*s underneath a stack of newspapers and kept my eyes on my shoes when she chastised the store owner for selling out of her favorite magazine. My bet was that my date hadn't read the book itself, but I didn't challenge him, more out of respect for Mr. Baines than anything else. He knew most of the people in the dining room, and they were all looking at us enough as it was. My mother drew their attention. She was dressed in clingy black crepe and stacked platform shoes. I contented myself with saying to my date, "That's your prerogative."

Then my mother did something that made things worse. She tried to change the subject, but in a way that would let my date know, indirectly, that he wasn't dealing with a yokel. Smiling sweetly at the young man, she said, "You know, Margaret's planning to attend Wellesley next term."

Although I was dying to ask her how she had narrowed the list down for me, I stayed quiet to wait for his response. He looked right at me, no shame at all, and asked whether I thought that was appropriate.

My mother, sweetly again, asked, "You mean because of the war?"

In a sneering, condescending sort of way he said, "No, not really." He wouldn't explain himself. He went back to his dessert.

What he meant was clear to my mother and me. He was asking whether it was appropriate for a middle-class Southern girl with no pedigree and no private tutelage to aspire to such a thing. If the conversation had continued, it would have deteriorated rapidly, punctuated by mean-spirited allusions to the fact that I had not made my debut, had not taken a European tour, had not mastered the gentle art of tea-pouring. I felt ill. My mother looked ill. Neither one of us could speak. Mr. Baines more or less defended my honor, going overboard in describing my abilities, and though I thought it ludicrous to be justified in such a manner, I felt relieved that someone was taking my part. I think that had I done it myself, I would've cried. I know my mother would've. When Mr. Baines finished quoting from the letter that had actually been sent to me by the admissions officer at Wellesley, the young man's face hadn't changed at all. There was still that arrogant smile of the sort Edward G. Robinson would've offered to wipe off his face.

My mother blurted out that it was late, we were tired, we needed the check and our coats, and the car pulled around front. The young man understood it was time to go. On the way home, my mother quizzed Mr. Baines on why he had set me up with this person. He agreed that the young man had shown himself, and he allowed that he must not be such a hot judge of character. My mother told him that she demanded to inspect my dates beforehand next time, and as the two of them discussed the particulars of how she'd meet the candidates for lunch and so on, I sat up, put my head between them, and said I'd had my last blind date.

My mother told me I was not giving up after one try. I told her I was. We yanked that around the rest of the way home, and then into and all through the house, long past midnight. The debate ended with my mother's stating her theory on why I lacked all the normal feminine interests. She said, "I know what's at the heart of all this business of your not wanting to date. It's your grandmother." Then she warned me to watch out or I'd get what I wanted. I'd grow old abnormal.

I told her that this was ridiculous and that I refused to talk about it anymore. However, when she went to bed I told my grandmother what had been said. She asked me whether I thought she was normal or abnormal.

She wasn't *abnormal*. That word described the old man who roamed about downtown, grabbing people by the sleeve, telling them the time, temperature, and current world news that had no connection to reality. Or the little girl we had just read about in the paper who wasn't sure of her age or name but could do fantastically long sums in her head. They were abnormal. My grandmother was certainly nothing like these two, but she wasn't normal in the sense of being like other people who worked in banks or stores, women with permanent waves and moisturized skin. But all the same, in the strangest sort of way, I considered her normal for herself. It was normal for her to eat two cloves of raw garlic every morning, wear her late mother's seventy-five-year-old shoes, preserve the laces in linseed oil, and sit up all night laughing uproariously over *Tristram Shandy*. I thought of all these things, and more, and said, "Well, you're not what I'd call abnormal, but you have done some things people might call odd."

"Yes, this is true," she said. "I have picked up a habit or two along the way. If I hadn't, I'd bore myself into the grave in about two days."

I did something very dangerous. I asked her whether she thought I'd be a spinster. "If I stay at home for another year or two and then get to college and compete with younger girls who've been raised in a more normal manner, will I lose out?"

She said, "Don't worry over it. You'll find your one-in-a-million, but you're sharp enough to know there's no point in sludging through the first nine hundred ninety-nine thousand, nine hundred ninety-nine to get to him. It may take you a while, but this isn't 1850. Your mother's not going turn you over to the workhouse or sell you to some man with a high starched collar and a whip." And then she said what she always said on those nights when she sat up in her bed sorting out my life for me: "Go to sleep."

My mother had been right in one regard, when she said to me all those times, *"Every young person is getting married, or just got married, or is looking to be married."* After Pearl Harbor, Raleigh seemed like a huge pocket turned inside out, shaking thousands of draftees and enlistees and their giddy brides out onto the train platform at the Seaboard Coast Line station. If I had cared to, all I would've had to do was walk out into the world with my hand out, ring finger ready. These were the years for standoffish wallflowers to step out from the wall and for the too heavy and the too thin to take a chance and put their feet forward as well. A sort of rabbity girl I had gone to school with stood absolutely no chance of marriage until she moved in with her sister in Norfolk and met a Navy enlistee who happened to go for her skittish type, and they were married quickly. They have enjoyed a long and happy life, or so it would seem from their holiday cards. In a port town such as Norfolk or Pensacola, shy stay-at-homes who closed their eyes and stepped out into the rush and thick of life probably found it all but impossible to stay single. Even the most mediocre seamstresses in port towns must have made mints overhauling Easter dresses, adding shoulder trains, and scalloping hemlines. Every magazine taught how to dye pumps and attach veils and Prince of Wales feathers to hats. The bottom requirement was that the couple like each other just a tad more than average. Prolonged court-ships were generally chopped off and pared down, so that a couple engaged on the first furlough was expected to be married on the second. As I overheard someone say, the world had never seen such marriages and multiplyings.

In October of 1942, I met Dr. Charles Nutter, whom I might have paid a nice sum to marry me had he not been twenty-seven years older and already married to a bright and truly kind woman whom he adored, pampered, and deserved. This idea aside, I more or less tortured myself with thoughts of how fine a father he would've been. He had just been appointed administrator of the Veterans Hospital in Durham when he called and invited my grandmother to volunteer for whatever nursing task suited her, promising her a highly coveted C gasoline ration card, free meals in the cafeteria, a uniform and orthopedic shoes. She didn't want to accept any of these things, but my mother finally persuaded her to take the priority card. She told her, "Senators' wives are scratching each other's eyes out over C cards. You should get it."

My grandmother called Dr. Nutter back and agreed to

work three days a week, and then, without consulting me, she said, "And I'll be bringing my granddaughter. Give her something to do, too." He was happy to have me, he said; he had heard regular reports of my academic work from my grandmother since I had been in first grade. He told her he would refer me to the hospital's Welfare and Recreation Office, which was run by his wife, Louise. I would be assigned to read and write letters for men who, for one sad reason or another, could not.

The next day I went to the hospital with my grandmother. Dr. and Mrs. Nutter met us at the front desk and offered a personal tour of the facility. My immediate thought was that my mother must have been out of her mind. The fact that she was a child was no excuse. She should've grabbed this man, tossed his larva buckets to the shore, and held his head underwater until he agreed to marry her. The idea that I had missed being his daughter was as devastating as if someone had told me, "You've heard of Henry James? Well, if your mother had played her cards right, she could've had him. Same thing with his brother, William. And you've heard of Emerson? Him, too. Same thing." Dr. Nutter seemed to have no flaws. He carried himself the way Franklin Roosevelt would have if it had not been for the polio. And somehow his voice had lost the odd Gullah quality common to people brought up on the far side of the Pasquotank. He sounded like the boy I knew who had gone to school at Lawrenceville Academy. They passed through the same sieve and came out sounding like Lowell Thomas.

He was respectful to my grandmother to the point of

doting, as was his wife, who said in so many words, "Miss Charlie Kate, if you'd not made him what he is, I wouldn't have met him. Thank you, thank you, thank you." Her family name was Battle. They were a very clannish group, more a tribe than a family, who were well-known in Raleigh for having descended from a proud and patriotic bunch of ancestors. But Louise was different. She had gone to New York to visit a college classmate, who introduced her around to women who were smoking, drinking straight liquor, and bobbing their hair, the sort of women who threatened to blow up the White House if that's what it took to get the vote. She came back South with a mission, being a new and avid member of the Transcendental Educational Society, the Women's Suffrage League, the Child Labor Law Association, and any other group that would improve the world and shock her parents simultaneously. In 1920 she traveled to San Francisco, unescorted, to the Democratic National Convention, and when she returned home she was hired by the State Board of Education to reduce North Carolina's thirty-percent illiteracy rate. From what my grandmother said, she was expected to do this single-handedly.

Louise met Dr. Nutter when he asked her to review the Dark Ages curriculum at his newly built Pasquotank Normal School. Almost immediately she felt a religious calling to move to Pasquotank County and lead its deprived children out of ignorance herself. Dr. Nutter was thrilled. So she moved into the back room of the school and spent the next two years marching dumbfounded students through Greek and Roman history, teaching boys the rudiments of home economics and girls the principles of hydraulics and chemistry. She spent her nights corresponding with her employer. Her proud and patriotic relatives were so horrified when she bypassed her debut to teach Pasquotank riffraff, trash, white niggers, and whatever else the children were called in supposedly good company, that they disowned her and had her name removed from the family pew at the Church of the Good Shepherd. Dr. Nutter learned about this and immediately increased Louise's salary. The episode strengthened their friendship, and soon they married, had twin boys, a girl, and more happiness and money and local fame than the local society pages could cover in their weekly updates on this family's life. They had three more children and adopted two migrant children, and bought a house as large as an orphanage and hosted an annual Easter Egg Roll on the front lawn in the manner of the President and First Lady.

It is worthwhile, cautionary, and simply interesting to report that Louise's parents lost every dime they had during the Depression. Charles bought the church pew for five hundred dollars, thereby allowing his in-laws to keep their house and automobile and thus some dignity. It is equally tragic to report that these scoundrels berated him when he restored their daughter's name to the brass plaque.

Two weeks before he called my grandmother, Dr. Nutter had been appointed hospital administrator, and his Horatio Alger story was told in newspapers from Richmond to Savannah. Not the entire story, of course, of the lunatic tubercular mother, or the disowned wife and the Episcopal pew, but enough to let the public know that its war-

wounded were in extraordinary hands. He gave my grandmother a generous share of the credit for his rise, and he
continued to do this as he introduced her around the hospital. This annoyed her greatly. "Stop slobbering over me,"
she told him. He did.

As we walked through the hospital wards, I saw a hundred or more men my age with nothing on but their pajamas, and in many cases just the bottoms. They seemed as
shaken by my presence as I was by theirs. If hands had
actually been roaming all over me, I could not have felt any
more, what a thing to say, felt. I flushed from all the eyes on
me. The wax fruit on my hat could very well have ripened.

Walking by one bed, my grandmother noticed the poor
drainage of a young man's leg. She reached down and
pressed the area around the wound and chastised Dr. Nutter for tempting gangrene or at the very least phlebitis. Then
she took the chart off the foot of the young man's bed and
noted that a morphine drip had been running continuously
since he was admitted. "Charles," she said, "this is gracious
of you not to let him suffer while you kill him."

Dr. Nutter blushed scarlet, saying he had not been aware
of the problem and that he would speak to the intern in
charge of this case immediately. Then he asked my grandmother if she thought the morphine should be discontinued.
She reached up and twisted the valve shut herself. She told
him to apply chaparral to the wound—a preparation he
would have to acquire from her famous herbalist friend
downtown. She gave him a list of other things she would
want available in the hospital pharmacy, all specific for

wounds: comfrey, echinacea, Saint-John's-wort, and aloe. He copied down the names of everything she needed, took five dollars out of his wallet, and sent an orderly on the errand downtown right away. Then he had iodine and bandages fetched so he could insert a proper drainage tube in the patient's leg himself, and he did so with his poplin suit on and trembling hands. He had the look of a child trying to tie his shoes correctly in spite of his mother's glaring-down eyes. And when he announced that he was finished, I turned around to see him searching my grandmother's face for approval, which she gave with a little grunt and a nod. It is not too much to suppose that he would have had a lousy rest of the day had her gesture not been forthcoming.

After he excused himself, a nurse got my grandmother started on her tasks, and Mrs. Nutter explained my duties to me. They didn't sound very complicated. I was to read the patients' mail, take their dictation, and then type the letters when I returned home and mail them the next morning. She told me it would be best not to pry into their affairs, as some of the volunteers had done. I was to remain friendly yet professional, keeping in mind that the men had had limited exposure to women for some time. I assured her that I knew how to handle myself, though had she known of my own limited exposure to young men she would have sent me home.

I was assigned two patients that morning, both injured when they were pitched onto the deck of their ships. One had been a gunner on a minesweeper that had been torpedoed, and up he went, fifteen feet in the air and then straight down onto the deck. His last clear memory was of other men being literally roasted to the deck, their skin hanging in shreds. He was very depressed and had been suffering blind spells which had been growing longer in duration; and if this wasn't grim enough, both his arms had been in plaster casts for three months and he wasn't sure he'd ever regain the full use of either. He was having intense psychological problems and was due to be evaluated for transfer to what Louise Nutter called the neuro ward.

She took me over to his bedside and introduced me. He would not talk or move or acknowledge my presence in any way. Before I could ask her what I was supposed to do, she said I'd find a pad and a pencil in his nightstand drawer, and she left. Do not think I'm heartless when I convey my honest reaction. It was: What am I supposed to do with this thing here? He lay on his side with his knees pulled up into his chest, his two plaster casts lying like snowy logs on top of his blanket. While I was trying to figure out what to say, I heard him.

"Open the goddamn drawer and read the letters," he said. His corrosive tone suggested that I had already offended him to the bone.

Through my grandmother I had met a fair sampling of pained individuals: alcoholics ranting with delirium tremens; women in labor shouting profanities at God and everybody; fevered people greeting dead relatives; and that one teenage boy who cursed violently and continuously, the one my grandmother had tried to spare from commitment to the asylum. All this is to say that I understood that people in pain could not be counted on to behave as if they were on a Sunday-afternoon stroll through the park. However, I didn't believe this patient was speaking to me entirely out of pain, and I wondered if he considered his pitiable condition a license to talk in this manner. I didn't expect deference, but I did expect civility. Also, there was the shock of being cursed by a stranger, and one I had come to help. It was then I realized that I had inherited my mother's and my grandmother's repugnance for people who will take incessantly, with ingratitude as their only returned favor. As at so many other times in my life, I thought about what my grandmother would say.

I said, "You can watch your mouth with me, or I'm going to take those plaster casts and shut them up in this drawer to which you so ill-temperedly referred."

If my grandmother had said this, it would have worked. I did not faze him. He said, "I told you to open the goddamn drawer and read the letters."

If he had had a knife to my throat he could not have sounded more threatening. I opened the drawer, and there lay a bundle of what seemed to be thirty or forty letters tied with a rawhide string.

I asked him if he intended for me to read all of them. He said he did. They looked to have been read many times. Their familiarity was no doubt soothing to him, but still I didn't think I should spend all this time with one patient. I told him I had another young man to work with, and that I would read the new, unopened letter on his nightstand. That was it.

Still curled in his ball, he said, "Then Goddammit, read it."

I opened the letter and read without thinking, without stopping. It was written in that loopy, childish hand that turns back on itself, a ridiculous style that indicated a frivolous girl who thought herself clever. The horror of my mistake was not revealed to me until I finished reading:

Dear Tab,

How are you? I wanted to drop you a little note and tell you something that's been on my mind, and that is I'm not going to go another day writing to you and saying everything's swell and we'll be swell when the opposite is true. What I want to say is that I don't think I should continue to wait. I'm not going to be eighteen forever and I feel like things are just slipping by and I'm missing them every single one. When you get right down and think about it can you actually blame me? You know how full of fun I've always been and how everybody's always talked about how I like to have a good time and, you know, just smell the roses. Don't think it has anything to do with your injuries and not knowing if you'll eventually be okay. And please don't think it has anything to do with another boy although I'd be cruel if I didn't say somebody I work with may come into the picture at a later date. He's a very special person and I bet if you were around him ten minutes you would think he's a real swell guy and you two would be real chums. This has just been so hard on me. I've hardly been able to concentrate on my work and they told me that if I keep messing up that it's back to Woolworth's for me. You know how I love my job and greeting the public and everything. Just don't think I'm letting you down.

Can you do me a big favor? You see, your mother has gone to lunch with mine a couple of times and things sort of got out of hand and they both took that bracelet for more than it is and, well, you know how mothers are these days with everybody getting married and everything. If you could sort of not mention this letter to your mother and then she won't mention it to mine and get everybody all upset and everything. That would be so swell of you. Just say something happened or something. That's what I'm going to do.

If you want to send my letters back I understand and I'll send back the friendship bracelet as soon as I find a little box for it.

Sincerely,
Arlene

He began to whimper. Then he started to sob and moan into his pillow. I sat by him because I thought it was the right thing to do. Watching him suffer was a sort of penance. I watched my tears fall and spread on my handbag, and I wondered when a nurse was going to come and throw me out. But nobody came. I guess the nurses were so used to seeing the patients' emotional states rotating from hope to despair and back again that another one's sobbing was no cause for alarm. I thought I should stay and clean up the mess I had made, as if I could piece a ruined life back together, as if I could touch him and coax him into saying that he would be fine and she wasn't the girl for him anyway. Had this been a movie, not only would he have done this, but he would've fallen in love with me and then a month later we would've laughed about the circumstances of our union. His hands and eyes would've been restored. He would've turned out to be wealthy beyond my dreams. We would've played rummy in the hospital sunroom until he was released and we could be married in grand style. But this wasn't a movie. This was a sour-smelling room of defeated young men sleeping on sheets circled with blood and urine that they wished their mother or sister or wife would come and change. Their idea of continuity and rhythm in life had become smoking cigarettes and waiting for mail. They had seen more in the past months than I could bear to imagine. I would never see anybody roasted to the deck of a burning ship thousands of miles from home.

What the patient said to me next wasn't true to any image from any movie. He said, "Go away. Go to hell."

I jumped up and ran for the ladies' room. I put the letter in my pocket, thinking another volunteer could come behind me and torture him all over again. From somewhere I heard a phonograph. Helen O'Connell was singing "Six Lessons from Madame LaZonga." I have loathed the song and the singer ever since.

I hid in the ladies' room for probably half an hour, rereading the letter, floored by this silly girl's cruelty, and mine. After a while, the dime-store paper, the envelope, the little blue-inked dollops of writing became despicable things in and of themselves, and for all my reading, I knew only now for the first time the power of a word. I was the accessory to a common crime of the day, but the fact that thousands of young men were receiving letters like this did not excuse me. It has been a matter of considerable regret that I was turned loose with the intimacies of another person's life when everything I knew about love I had learned from watching my mother and Mr. Baines and from reading Edith Wharton, whose characters rarely managed to get it right. Part of me wanted to turn myself in at the nurses' station and say to them, "I am young and ignorant and foolish. Therefore, I am going home."

It took everything I had for me to come out of the ladies' room and meet the other patient. I remember wondering whether I could redeem myself with him. I peeked into the ward and saw the first young man still curled on his side. Had I had more experience or common sense or wisdom I would have braved apologizing to him, but, I am ashamed to say, I did not. He was transferred to the neuro ward soon after this. How many times have I told myself that it was not my fault, that he was full of problems already? On a later visit I passed him in the hall, shuffling along in old-man slippers, his robe stained, his hair matted, a glassy-eyed lost boy leaning on the arm of a fat nurse. I let him have a good look at me, my spontaneous and thoroughly feeble attempt to give him permission for revenge, but he stared straight through me. I seemed to have been forgotten. Everything seemed to have been forgotten.

The next young man appeared pleasant, exceptionally pleasant for someone missing both arms up to the elbows.

His eyes were not bandaged, but he told me he felt he was looking at me through thick gauze. I didn't ask him any personal questions, but he volunteered that he was the baby of the family and that his mother had gladly sent her three sons to the Navy in spite of the deaths of the Sullivan boys, five brothers in one family who had been killed in the Pacific. He was from Lumberton, a nearby town, and his mother came and read to him every other Sunday. As she read, she fed him little broken pieces of peanut brittle. A round red tin with a Currier and Ives scene on the lid and a library copy of *Daniel Boone: The Pioneer Scout* were on his nightstand. I imagined that outside of the outright death of a child, a mother could experience no sight more pitiful than the baby of her family missing an arm or a leg, missing anything, really.

He was anxious to dictate a letter to his mother. He lay back with his chin up, his bandaged elbows up by his ears. He closed his eyes to help concentrate his mind. He was such a nervous, twitchy person, scratching one half an arm and then the other into his side. He would dig hard, gouging, actually. It was disturbing, and I wondered why this was not hurting him. The sight went completely through me. Once he settled down, he began dictating the letter. He seemed to speak directly to his mother:

Dear Mom,
    This is very important. Okay? You know my suits? I've been thinking about them a lot. They've been in the hall closet since I gave Joseph my room, and do

you know what? The moths will eat them whole. I want you to go in there and apply this new product called Larvex to them. Okay? Remember, L-A-R-V-E-X. The stuff kills the moths before they're big enough to go after a suit of clothes. Okay?

One of the night nurses told me if she had enough time tonight she would read to me, since you can't come Sunday. If she does, it won't be the same. When we finish this book, can you please bring something about the life and times of Davy Crockett? You know how Daniel Boone will put a fellow to thinking of Davy Crockett. Please tell everyone hello and don't worry about me. Just don't forget about the Larvex. Okay?

Your son,

Frank

After the letter to his mother, he said he wanted to write his sister in Georgia to tell her about the moth product. He was very intent on spreading the word around to his family. He spoke as if, from his hospital bed, he was protecting them from some menace. He even said to me, "Say! Do you use Larvex?"

I told him that I did, and that it worked wonderfully, just as he described. That seemed to please him. Telling him what he wanted to hear, I suppose, was kind of a ragtag redemption. After we wrote his sister, I asked him what he wanted to do. He said, "What I really want to do is read that book."

I told him I would read a chapter. He showed an eager boy's gratitude, and he burrowed himself down in his covers to listen. He stopped his wretched scratching. I remember the first line of the chapter: "Daniel Boone's mind was as sharp as his hatchet." The young man's eyes were closed, and his face showed the contentment of one who had retreated far to the rear, far back with a mother whose bountiful heart allowed her to sit for three hours on Sundays reading a boys' book to her boy. I bet she was the kind of mother who would've dropped everything, yanked off her apron and thrown it in the corner to rush to the hardware store for Larvex, and harassed the clerk when he couldn't locate it on the shelf. I bet she sat up at night and read and reread letters from her baby, which is how she would've thought of him, crying both in pain for his loss and with relief that the war, for him, was over. He had such a sweet face, the delicate features of a young girl, the longest eyelashes in the world.

On the way home from the hospital I told my grandmother about the two patients. She said something incredible. She suggested that I write the first one's girlfriend even though I had been told not to do so, and then correct several impressions the second boy had made.

I asked her what sorts of impressions.

She said, "Those regarding his reason." Then she said, "You have to ask yourself if these young men would be better served by your writing the truth as you know it or the truth as they think they see it or wish it to be. If you had a son in the hospital and got an obsessive letter about moths, would it be good for you or bad?"

I said that it would be bad, that I would worry.

She said, "And he's going to mend nicely. All the sparrows will leave his head. All his reason will return. Why not give his mother a break from worry? Do you see the point?"

I saw the point. I trusted my grandmother. Everything she had ever said had been true, and I had long since learned to do whatever she told me to do. Trusting her to guide me in this circumstance was like falling backward like her chloroformed women, knowing that not only would I be caught, but I would be caught before I realized I was falling.

We arrived back home that afternoon on the heels of my mother, who had just returned from having thrown half of the Raleigh Junior League out of the Red Cross workroom for what she termed their "ignorance and insubordination, both individually and as a group." My mother's job was assigning daily tasks, and that day she had instructed the workers to pull threads in sheets, cut long strips, or roll already cut strips into bandages. The regional office gave her weekly quotas to fulfill, and she had already earned several certificates of merit for surpassing the quotas. But this time the workers fell into such an uproar over their assignments that she finished the day with only about twenty percent of the requirement met. It was my understanding that some of the women could become territorial over these tasks, and that the Junior Leaguers and society idlers felt they were too often assigned to pull threads. There was (phenomenal to report) some prestige in using the scissors and rolling the bandages. The women brought their complaints to my mother, implying that they needed to be treated with a certain deference. My mother told us, "We all argued into a fight. Even the woman who accused another woman of snatching her scissors teamed up against me."

My grandmother asked what happened next. She loved sporting stories, particularly boxing stories by Ring Lardner, and this tale had all that kind of potential. She said, "Did they call each other names?"

My mother told her that hadn't happened. She said she told the women to leave and go knit socks for Stalingrad, and then one of them assured my mother that she'd be hearing from her husband. My mother, knowing exactly how gorgeous and smart she was, and how threatening to women like these, announced, "That would be fine with me! I'm home most evenings." The women herded themselves together like lambs and left.

That night after supper, when my mother had had a chance to calm down, the three of us sat at the kitchen table with my typewriter, Arlene's letter, and the one the Lumberton boy had dictated to me. My mother and grandmother read them through several times. After a few minutes, my grandmother said, "I know exactly what to say to the girl. Get ready and take this down."

She began to speak, but my mother interrupted and told her she was concerned that this might be mail fraud.

My grandmother said, "What? What do you think? Hugo's going to arrest you at the post office?"

My mother thought about Hugo a moment. He presented no danger. He was just a tiny old man who sold stamps and money orders and who had never learned to count change.

Sometimes he got lucky, but usually he slid a mix of coins back across the counter and looked away while the customer slid back what was necessary or, if it wasn't enough, said, "Excuse me, Hugo, but I need another nickel." Hugo would flush and apologize, chalking the error up to his tendency to think in foreign money. He had taken a Cuban holiday as a young man, and he spent the rest of his life trying to learn Spanish.

This is what my grandmother dictated, stopping every couple of lines to wink at me. It was a grand curse:

> Dear Arlene,
>   It is a sorry girl who spits upon one fallen. The rest of your life will be hopeless and worthless, and you will see me everywhere you wander. And wander you will, from dolt to dimwit until you find the one of your dreams, or in your case, your nightmares. May your children inherit your husband's scoliosis, clubfeet, recessed testicles, or whatever else has kept him out of the fighting. As for the bracelet, throw it off the first bridge you see. As for my sight, I can see what you are. As for my hands, I'm glad they're off you.
>   Thanks for nothing,
>   Tab

My grandmother was enormously proud of this. She and my mother laughed out loud and had me read it back several times.

My grandmother said, "Type his name to it, and be grateful his hands are bound up so he can't sign it."

Writing the letter was intrusive and audacious, but it was also a thoroughly practical and seemingly harmless method of vengeance. And there was the matter of getting caught, which in and of itself was rather titillating, as illicit actions naturally are. But I put myself in Arlene's shoes. Would I write back? Certainly not. I knew she'd never find a little box for that friendship bracelet. I thought she'd keep it in her cheap white ballerina jewelry box, which I suspected she owned, for the two weeks or so it would take her to distance herself from uncomfortable memories, and then she would either wear it and lie about where it came from or give it to a little sister or cousin who would lose it at the playground. Either way, she would feel nothing, or at best, little. Therefore she deserved the letter, even though it wouldn't shame her. I believed it would embarrass her, though, shame and embarrassment being different only in the degree to which her cheeks would redden and her stomach would churn; and she would tear it up so her mother wouldn't find it and make her confront the guilt she had long since put in a little box and tied, taped, or nailed shut.

My grandmother told me to roll in another sheet of paper. "We're going to do the Larvex boy," she said. She then recited what she believed he would believe to be the truth if it were not for the sparrows:

Dear Mom,
I hope everything's fine with you today. I'm better, and I want you to know that even though I'll miss you on Sunday, I'll be okay. It has meant the world to me,

having you come every other week and read. Some of the fellows here haven't had a visitor since they got here, and I can tell you they're certainly jealous of me. Do you know what your visits remind me of? They remind me of when I was just a little guy and the way you read to me all the time. That sort of thing sticks with a fellow, and I can't tell you how much that memory meant to me when I was at sea. You certainly are the best mom a guy could ever have.

I need to close now, but I want to let you know one more time what a swell mom you are. And one more thing. Can you please bring a book about Davy Crockett the next time you come? It would be interesting to compare his experiences in the wilderness to Daniel Boone's.

Love,
Frank

My grandmother thought this was splendid. I did, too, especially his memory of having been read to as a boy. Everything was designed to make his mother feel better about what had happened. I imagined her reading it, going upstairs to his room, sitting down on his twin bed, no doubt with a cowboy-and-Indian bedspread on it, and crying her eyes out, a good cathartic cry. I liked her immensely. I imagined her bosom wet with her tears, her house perpetually the odor of pine cleanser and peanut brittle, the walls papered in worn trompe l'oeil, her shoes a little down in the heel because she didn't like to spend money on herself.

After my grandmother sealed the two letters for me to address and stamp, she put her feet up on her ottoman and did what, sadly enough, she was spending more and more time doing lately. She read aloud the names of that week's enlistees in the newspaper, remarking on the ones she had delivered, telling us what a big baby this one had been or how jaundiced another had been. She would say, "It was very rough. I remember how it was raining when I got there. I remember how the other children played at my feet." She had delivered many of my classmates. When the list of combat fatalities started to swell, she would read these names aloud also, and when I recognized them, I didn't think of the young men as ensigns or privates or whatever else they had been when they died. I thought of them as the boy who picked his nose during the senior play or the boy who was caught with French verbs conjugated on his sleeve or the boy who tried to abandon his date at the dance, the one whose wingtips my grandmother had stood on. He died early in the war, having enlisted at the first chance he had. So did the boy who could not for the life of him remember that Samuel Clemens and Mark Twain were the same person and who spoke of this as if it were a conspiracy to confuse him.

I mailed the two letters the next morning. It started snowing that day about noon, a great, blowing snow that stuck, a rarity in the Piedmont of North Carolina. By late in the day, we had six inches of snow. Mr. Baines left work early and risked his neck driving the unplowed roads to our house, no doubt because he knew he wouldn't be able to get back into town after sunset. He walked with us down the road to a going-away party for a boy named Nathaniel, who was due to leave for training camp the following morning. I remember the gift we brought, a tooled leather wallet with a five-dollar bill inside.

Nathaniel had been two years ahead of me in high school, and although we had lived down the road from each other all our lives, he had never said more than a handful of words to me. He would get on the school bus with his head down, sit by himself, and gaze out the window. He was crippled by shyness. He never went forward to receive his perfect-attendance certificates at school. He'd just sit there when his name was called, and I could see the principal laying the certificate to the side, thinking, Oh yes, he's the shy boy. Whenever I spoke to him, his face would suddenly become blotchy, as if I had reached out and slapped him hard on both cheeks. I could all but hear his heart pounding in his throat. A couple of times his mother sent him to our house to borrow things, and he'd blurt out what he'd come for, snatch it, and run like a thief back across our yard.

His father bullied him into enlisting, for all the usual reasons—to put hair on his chest, to make a man out of him, to stop him from being a sissy. His mother forced this reception on him for the same reason she had organized birthday parties he didn't want. She meant to bring him out of himself. His father chose that night to bring him out of himself also, pouring mint juleps into his son, making him so sick that he vomited, fell while running to the bathroom, vomited again, fell again, and then repeated the process until he was finally down the hall with the bathroom door shut behind him. My grandmother went after him and made him let her in. She stayed with him in the bathroom for an hour, fending off his parents at the door, saying, "You caused him to heave, now let him heave!" I remember my mother's whispering into my ear: "Now we know why the South lost the war."

This was the first time Mr. Baines spent the night at our house. My mother made a big show of fixing up the guest room for him, knowing all the while that as soon as my grandmother and I were asleep either she or Mr. Baines would take a trip down the hall. Many times before, he had stayed until he believed we were asleep. I would hear him and my mother sneak down the hall, and an hour or two later I would hear them sneak back the other way, and then hear the door shut and his car start. My grandmother rolled her eyes at all the commotion of fluffing pillows and adjusting the radiator, telling me, "Why they haven't slipped up yet is beyond me. He must be fixed."

The next day it snowed again. Mr. Baines was stranded at our house for the duration. My mother was gleeful. They could play house. My grandmother and I couldn't drive the thirty minutes to the hospital, so we hung about and watched my mother leading him through all the activities she believed a happy modern couple would do together. They used up all the rationed sugar to bake cookies. They used all the cream to make eggnog, and all the molasses to make a ginger cake. They danced in broad daylight, and mixed martinis for the lot of us and served them in our best crystal.

It was like being at camp for adults. My mother would sip her martini and gaze out the window, wishing for more snow.

Lassiter Mill Pond was frozen again, and when my mother and Mr. Baines had run out of things to do indoors, they announced that they were taking the dining room chair back out there. My grandmother told them that this was foolish and dangerous and that their reason had been distorted by what she called their "unrelenting boozing before sunset." She doubted the pond was frozen hard and deep enough to support their weight. They went anyway. I got my grandmother's coat and the two of us followed them to the car, my grandmother telling Mr. Baines as she crawled into the backseat, "Somebody needs to be there to pull you two out." I wasn't so much worried about the ice's cracking and taking them under as curious to see my mother in full motion on the pond, legs up and head back.

The frozen pond did support them, and the exhilaration my mother felt came to me, it seemed, in a correspondent breeze of the sort Wordsworth wrote about. It filled my chest, all my mother's happiness blown directly into me. This was also happening to my grandmother. I could tell by the way she stared at them. I imagined her memories of watching my mother as a child, sitting at the kitchen table with her Blueback Speller, learning hard words with such joyous ease. I imagined my grandmother's memories of all the times my mother had pleased her, supremely. This was one of those times.

The old man who shined shoes at Poole's Pie Parlor

appeared at the pond, with a bucket, a pole, and a camp stool. He stood at the edge of the pond, looked over to my grandmother and me and waved, and then pointed to my mother and Mr. Baines to let us know he thought they were a fine sight. We waved back to let him know we felt the same. Then he proceeded out toward the center of the pond, and when he was no more than four feet away from the bank, the ice cracked and he went down quickly, as if something underwater had jerked him hard by his pants leg. All four of us fell into motion. Mr. Baines got the jumper cables from his car, ran and lay on the side of the pond, and tossed one end of the cables into the hole. My grandmother took off her coat and instructed my mother and me to do the same.

Two young women, exquisitely dressed for a weekday walk on the path beside the pond, came over to watch. My grandmother looked at them for the few seconds it took her to realize that they weren't going to offer their coats and she wasn't going to waste her energy begging them. And then she stood by Mr. Baines's feet, clapping her hands together, shouting in rhythm as she clapped, "Take it! Take it!" After the miserable eternity of three or four minutes, we saw hands at the top of the ice. We all yelled for the man to hang on as Mr. Baines pulled him with the cable, hand over hand, to the bank.

When the man was safely out of the water, my grand-mother fell to work on him. She tucked our coats around him, and then tilted his head back, ran her finger around inside his mouth, tilted his head back even farther, and checked his throat. When she took her finger out, it was coated with wadded plant matter, which she shook off over to her side, directly onto the stocking of one of the onlookers. The woman hissed, "Oh, please," and borrowed a handkerchief from her companion to wipe her leg. My grandmother got down on her knees behind the man's head and told Mr. Baines to ride his chest and pump it between her blows. She put her mouth over the old man's. She and Mr. Baines worked on him for another miserable eternity; finally his eyes opened and he coughed until my grandmother told him to stop before his throat became too raw. She told him how to breathe. "Look at me," she said. "Do what I do. You have to get back in charge of yourself."

The two women left. They ambled back along the path. It was as if they had just watched handlers unloading animals off a circus train and one of them had accidentally stepped in something unpleasant. Did they go home and tell their husbands? Did they dream about it? For years after this incident, thinking about the two of them caused a neuralgia to grip my neck and shoulders that could be mitigated only by imagining them trapped in unhappy homes with husbands, children, pets, and servants who bristled when they passed.

We took the old man home to his wife and thousand children, and my grandmother promised to visit him with medicine later that day, and the next day and the next, until he was out of danger of pneumonia. I could not imagine a gratitude more sincere unless it was that she had received from the hanging man. When we got home, Mr. Baines went right in and fixed a drink for himself and my mother. I wanted one dearly, and so did my grandmother, who told Mr. Baines not to be stingy when he poured for her. She took the glass from him and justified, as if she ever needed to justify anything to herself, a drink in the afternoon. "Somewhere on this planet," she said, "it is five o'clock."

The man she resuscitated became a religious zealot. Starting the next Sunday at the A.M.E. Zionist church and continuing until his death, he dedicated and rededicated his life to Jesus. It was said that during his loud and long testimonials he would recount the way my grandmother had pressed her mouth to his and saved his life. People never tired of hearing the tale. It enjoyed wide circulation, spilling out of his church and onto the streets, where it called up memories of the miracle of the lynched man. Had my grandmother not delivered the local leader of the Klan and sent him birthday cards and nickels and the pamphlet that spared him from pubescent fatherhood, I'm sure we would've awakened some night to find a blazing cross in our yard.

Dr. Nutter called each day to keep my grandmother up-to-date on several of the young men she had been concerned about. Although the hospital was greatly understaffed because of the weather, he made her promise she wouldn't chance the drive to Durham. We didn't get back there for six days, which was exactly how much time it took for a letter to reach Lumberton and a reply to reach the hospital by special delivery.

I went straight to Frank's bedside when I got to the hospital. A letter from his mother was waiting on his nightstand. I read it through to myself before reading it aloud to him, unpleasant previous experience being the best teacher around. I saw from the letter that he had been adopted at age thirteen. His mother was concerned that the blow to his head had jiggled his memory. So much for his tender memory of this woman's reading to him when he was a small boy. I realized that my grandmother's plan for me to tell the truth as I believed the young men wished it to be could prove a very complicated business. I edited the letter as I read along. This is not what he heard:

Dear Frank,

Thank you so much for your lovely letter. I am so happy to know that you're in good spirits and that my not coming on Sunday has not made you blue. I hope you were able to enjoy the snowfall outside of your window. Lumberton was a blanket of white, and all the schoolchildren spent the day on the hill behind our house.

There was one thing that disturbed me about your letter, though. Honey, I know this is such a painful time for you and that it would be natural to look back on the past and try and make things a way they never were. Although we've never talked too much about your adoption, I thought you would clearly remember coming to us on your thirteenth birthday. Remember the cake and the red bike we had waiting for you? You know that with all my heart I wish that I had read to you when you were small. If new memories for the old bad ones help you now, then I won't worry. My only concern was that the trauma related to the explosion has caused some emotional disturbances. That was my only concern. Otherwise, honey, you sound so much better.

I'll see you next Sunday. Do you think you'd like for me to bring snapshots? We could tape them to the side of your nightstand. I'll certainly bring the Davy Crockett book from the library.

All my love,
Mom

After I finished reading everything except the lines concerning his adoption, he said, "Boy, that was a short one."

He sounded so disappointed that I rattled the envelope and told him there was another letter inside, and as he lay there with, lucky for me, his eyes closed, I spun the best story I could about all the wonderful snow in Lumberton, how it had shone silver under the streetlights, how everyone was sad that it wouldn't linger until Christmas. He was perfectly satisfied when I finished, but I was a wreck, having jumped off the roof of my sheltered life straight down into someone else's. I felt as if I had this boy's life all over me, and I had no idea how to extricate myself. I could see myself thirty years from then, driving to Lumberton every day to intercept letters between Frank and his mother. Where this would take me, how it would end, I had no idea. As I readied myself for his dictation, I tried but could not shake the image of me at fifty, hiding behind a tree, waiting for her mailman to come, eventually being caught and dragged off to tell a true-crime tale of good intentions gone berserk that would horrify everyone in the world, except possibly my mother and grandmother, who would come to my trial and proudly testify, "To have done it so well for so long—how grand!"

I WAS ASSIGNED to another patient that first day back after the snowfall. He was from Mississippi, a place I was highly interested in, not only because I liked William Faulkner but also because I was at that time reading Eudora Welty's *A Curtain of Green.* Right away I asked the young man a thousand questions about the Delta. Like so many people away from home, he was eager to tell me all about it, everything he missed: the cool black loam, the cool well water, the cool breeze his mother prayed aloud for before every summer supper. He asked me if I'd like to hear about his mom and pop. I told him I would. I listened carefully, as I knew the information would stand me in good stead if, or rather when, correspondence needed to be concocted. As he talked to me, I thought of how thoroughly normal my grandmother would seem in his world, even with her mothball-scented body and garlic-scented breath and antique pantaloons.

169

When he was growing up, his father had tended bar at a place called the Bucket of Blood Saloon. The man was a hard character, a severe alcoholic whose paychecks flew from his hands. To get spending money, the boy and his little brothers would go to the city maintenance lot near their home and pick change out of the dirt that was swept from the streetcars each week, and to make grocery money his mother kept retired plow horses in the backyard and rented them out when her neighbors had a call for them. They usually hired them to pull their possessions from house to house, trying to beat rent during the Depression, a time he described as his mother's heyday. This mother never let her children ride the animals while they were alive, but as soon as an old horse died she would call her children out of the house and they'd all crawl up on top as the animal was hauled away. What a vision he was making for me!

Also, he told me that his mother lived for the parish lottery. He remembered her waking up one morning, screaming that she had dreamed of clear water, then rushing out of the house, still in her nightgown, to play the numbers 1, 2, and 3, which were specific for dreams of clear water. I expected him to say next that his mother lost the money, his father came home drunk and beat her and the children, and they all ate chickpeas for supper. Instead, he beamed and said that she won fifty dollars, bought a new icebox and filled it with food, and bought all the children new shoes. In spite of redeeming times like that, his life didn't sound like anything to do a jig over.

I remember that as I listened to him my eyes would

wander up over his bed, where a crucifix was displayed upon which hung a Christ wearing what looked to be horsehair, or worse I feared, and a muslin wrap held together by a diaper pin. The look on His face was not so much the usual agony as surprise. (To this day, I have yet to see the Savior depicted with his mouth open to that extent, all his teeth showing.) His mother had sent it with an outsize birthday card, which was taped to the wall open for everyone to read. She had written:

> I and the Most Blessed Holy of Holies wish you a Speedy Recovery. A Mass was said for you last Sunday but it wasnt attended so hot on account of everybody used their gas coupons Getting Drunk Saturday Nite as is the comin rule these days but Not To Worry Father Benet said its not so much the number of prayers that go up anyway as it is The Speed And The Heart behind them. You shud have seen your Mama All Dolled Up craning her head around backwards to see Who was coming to Pray for her Baby. I had on the hat you sent me from Guam Plus the earbobs.

The young man was recuperating from a massive skin-grafting procedure; he had been burned mightily on his chest and stomach in a boiler accident on his ship. He needed my assistance because he was illiterate. He seemed bright enough to have absorbed something from school, even if his home life had erased his slate each evening. He debated the fellow in the bed next to his over Mr. Roosevelt's support of the soldier vote, and he followed all the comic strips by reading the pictures only, just as I had done as a child. So I felt compelled to ask him why he hadn't learned to read and write. (One must bear in mind that one Southerner can ask another Southerner this with little fear of recrimination, as long, of course, as it isn't asked in a condescending manner. Had he heard New Jersey or even Baltimore in my accent, he would've told me to mind my own affairs.)

When I asked about his illiteracy, he shrugged and told me, "Like I said, I'm from Mississippi."

I said, "Do you mean that as an excuse?"

He laughed and said something to the effect that nobody in Mississippi could read or write.

I asked him if he had heard of William Faulkner. He asked me who he was.

I said, "He happens to be a Mississippian who reads and writes very nicely. He writes about a place called Yoknapatawpha."

He told me there was no such place, that he had been everywhere in Mississippi, and then I explained that Faulkner had created and populated it in his imagination. The patient seemed content enough with the explanation, and so I moved on. I asked if he was ready to dictate a letter home. He said he didn't want to. I showed him the stack of letters he had been fortunate enough to receive recently, and he said, "Mom *made* them write me." Her parish was involved in a letter-writing campaign to servicemen, and he seemed to have gotten the bulk of their efforts. I could see this woman lording over card tables of women in a church

172

fellowship hall, making sure her boy got more than his due.

When I pressed him to tell me why he wouldn't send anything home, he asked, "What's there to say except my temperature's ninety-nine and I haven't had a b.m. on my own yet?"

I said, "Granted, that isn't big news, but you should send something home anyway."

He said if I really wanted to do him a favor, I would send his mother last Sunday's funny pages, but I was first to clip out *Little Orphan Annie*. Daddy Warbucks made her crazy. Like my grandmother, she considered him a hate-spreading Republican of the Hoover variety and spoke of him as if he were real. I agreed to do this, and then I read him all the letters from the parishioners. In the main, they were nothing more than form letters. It seemed as if the women had copied down a letter put before them on a blackboard.

When I finished, I excused myself and went to find my grandmother. She was changing the dressing on a nasty burn on a patient's thigh, telling him how lucky he was that it wasn't closer to his crotch. I sat down by her and told her about the Bucket of Blood, the crucifix, and the way the young man hadn't been able to place Yoknapatawpha. She nodded as she folded the dressing and taped it down, and then she squeezed the patient's knee and said, "This one's from Pittsburgh. From what I hear about Pittsburgh, half the people there'd prefer it was something made up in somebody's head. Am I correct?" He understood he was to agree, so he did.

He was her last patient of the day. She had been assigned

two aisles, and she had finished them both, working at top speed so she could have lunch with Dr. Nutter in his office. I had one more patient left. We agreed to meet after she was through with lunch. Before I went into my ward, I noticed on the next patient's information card that he was from Raleigh. Although he was a graduate of Washington and Lee, he was a noncommissioned officer. His name was Tom Hawkings III. He was recovering from surgery performed aboard a hospital ship to remove shrapnel from his back, and his right hand was splinted. His condition was listed as excellent.

His family was well-known, as was their residence. The house was based on Monticello, only it was larger. The Hawkings family lived across the street from the doctor whom my grandmother had retired. Their name was particularly fresh in my mind, as I had read just a few months before about the three Hawkings sisters who were married in a lavish triple ceremony. Their father owned the largest office supply firm in the state, and every now and then he received mention in the business pages for having acquired another furniture store or shoe store or grocery store. The patient's mother had written the "Under the Dome" political column in the Raleigh newspaper for the past ten years or so, and she was often listed as a speaker at teas and book club and alumni meetings. The younger son was always getting his picture in the paper for hanging about at high-tone New York social events with the Daniel boy, also from Raleigh, who later married Margaret Truman. And the one sister who didn't get married in the triple ceremony was famous for being the first resident of Raleigh to attend Juilliard. Why someone like this Tom Hawkings III didn't have a commission puzzled me. Either he had unconventional, highly democratic ideals or was trying to prove something to his overachieving family, or there was simply something wrong with him.

I couldn't tell, not right away. He was asleep on his stomach when I got to him, and when I touched his shoulder and told him it was mail time, he shooed me away. He actually said, "Shoo!" His card had also stated that he was ambulatory. He wasn't supposed to be sleeping during the hours reserved for welfare and recreation activities. Dr. Nutter was very strict about patients' participating in recreational therapy to fend off depression. If a patient was confined to bed, he was to be awake, and those not confined were to be up and about, occupying their minds in the dayroom, playing cards for matchsticks, painting-by-number, reading magazines, things like that. When I asked why several of the beds had no mattresses, I was told that orderlies sometimes removed the ambulatory patients, along with their mattresses, from the beds for the activity hour and put them both back afterward. I leaned down toward the patient's ear and told him I had been assigned to him and intended to stay as long as it took. There was no response, so I pulled a chair by his bed and sat there, waiting for him to wake up or for my grandmother to finish her lunch with Dr. Nutter, whichever came first.

I sat there twenty minutes or so and finally asked a nurse what I should do. She told me he was an especially difficult case, and she was eager to tell me exactly why. The subject of Tom Hawkings III exercised her so much that her eyes bugged and her nostrils flared when she spoke. She started with how the staff had threatened to dump him out of bed, but they had backed down when they realized he'd just crawl up on the springs and go back to sleep. That's how stubborn he was. She told me he'd sleep on nails if that was all the mattress he had. The other patients were treated by residents and interns, but he was treated by Dr. Nutter himself. The nurse said, "That was his *mother's* doing." Dr. Nutter had just taken him off codeine, but the patient swore he still hurt like crazy and the only relief he had was sleep. "So," she said, "there he is, twenty-four hours a day. Waking up when he pleases and doing as he pleases." The other fellows who had had the same surgery on the same day didn't hurt anymore, so why should he? She suggested I skip him. I should boycott him, the way the rest of the staff did, and save myself a ton of frustration. Then she added, "Well, everybody but these colored orderlies ignores him. He bribes them to bring him milk shakes from the hamburger stand downtown and ham biscuits from their mamas' houses. They line up to fetch for him. Yesterday he paid one of them a dollar to leave work and go buy him a cheese-burger. You could smell it all over this ward, and when the other fellows whined about it, you know what he did? He sent the colored guy back out for twenty more. I'll be glad when he's out of here."

I didn't boycott him. I couldn't leave the side of someone described to me in terms I'd always applied to my grandmother. I wanted to know more about him, and so I sat there and scrutinized him, noting the moles on the top of his shoulders and the way his thigh muscles flinched underneath the sheet every now and then. He was exposed to his waist. His head was turned to the side, and his arms were raised up and crossed underneath his pillow. He was a supremely good-looking individual of the caliber one rarely encounters. His hair was black, though already salted at the temples with gray. There was nothing about him that wasn't a pleasure to behold. He had truly excellent features, perfect skin, a perfect nose. His mouth was open just a little, and I know that had my grandmother been by my side, she would've goaded me into lifting his lip to check his teeth. I guessed they were white and straight. Thick black hair was starting to grow again on his back. With all that hair, it must've taken somebody an hour to shave him, and he was still covered in razor nicks. The tracks of stitches all over him caused me to imagine a crazy person standing over him, scribbling wildly on him with purple and black ink. He was still bruised around the incisions. I understood why he hurt.

I wanted to touch him. I remember feeling suddenly conscious of my arms. My muscles tightened and prepared to move without my consent, automatically—a response of the sort mothers have when they put on brakes and reach over to hold their children back even after the children are grown and gone. The urge to move toward him spread all over me, head to toe. I think it had a great deal to do with the way the sheet lay across the small of his back.

My grandmother appeared beside me. She said, "What's

wrong with him? Charles doesn't like it when these boys sleep all day."

I let her read his card. She handed it back to me, saying, "He needs to get up."

I defended him on the basis of what I knew of him from his naked back and the side of his face. "Let's leave him alone," I said. "If he's this tired, he must have a reason."

She ignored me and shouted into his ear, "Son! Wake up! Stay up all night and sleep all day! How do you ever expect to get well?"

Tom Hawkings III woke up, lifted his head of unruly hair, and asked my grandmother what time it was and also would she get him some orange juice and dry toast. He murmured, "That'd be swell of you." I wondered whether he was just waking from a dream that had him back in Anderson Heights on a Saturday morning. The maid was staying late on her day off to fix his breakfast exactly the way he wanted it, and his father was out in the yard, killing time, waiting for him to wake up so he could ask him how he'd put so many miles on the Buick the night before. Nothing in Tom's calm voice said he realized he was on a ward with twenty other young men and that his back was a mess from having been sprayed with shrapnel four weeks before.

My grandmother said, "I didn't come here to be *swell*." He twisted his head around and looked at me, saying with his eyes, Then will *you* do it for me?

My grandmother said, "She didn't come to be *swell*, either. Wake up and write a letter to your mother. That's what would be *swell*." (I must tell how a short time before this, while listening to a radio essay about Mr. Roosevelt's Four Freedoms, later trivialized by Mr. Rockwell and *The Saturday Evening Post,* my grandmother shouted, "They forgot about the Fifth Freedom!" My mother asked what that could be. My grandmother said, "Freedom from hearing the word 'swell.' You can't go to the toilet without somebody telling you something's *swell.*")

Tom pushed himself up on his elbows, grimacing as he did, and asked my grandmother if she'd like to write his mother.

My grandmother said, "That's what I'll do. I'll write her and say her son's lazing off at the Veterans Hospital when he ought to be up trying to exercise."

He laid his head back down and said, "Go on and do it. Tell her Tom's assing off again. Send it to Anna Hawkings, care of the *News and Observer.*"

My grandmother said, "Okay. That's what we'll do."

She left the bedside. He asked me what she was up to.

I took a box of stationery out of his nightstand drawer and told him she had probably gone to find an extra chair to drag over so she could be more comfortable while he dictated a letter to me. I said, "She tends to do what she says she'll do. If I were you I'd be careful." I noticed a German edition of *The Magic Mountain* on his table, and I asked him if all these patients with their hacking, tubercular-sounding coughs put him in mind of Hans Castorp.

He smiled and asked me if I'd read it. I told him I had, in translation.

I was afraid he'd say something snide about reading a

translation, but he didn't. He asked, "Who *are* you two?"

I told him my name and my grandmother's, and when he heard hers, he sighed and flattened himself out on his stomach and said, "That's just swell. Mom's hero's here to torture me."

My grandmother arrived with a chair while I was asking him to explain himself. He craned his neck around to speak to her. He said she had scored all sorts of points with his mother for putting their neighbor out of business.

My grandmother asked how his parents knew this secret.

He replied, "Mom knows everything." Then he said that if he wrote a letter saying he'd met my grandmother, his mother might loosen up on him a bit. She'd been nagging him about not assisting in his recovery. "The Nutters squealed on me," he said.

My grandmother told him to start talking. She told him not to worry about my ability to keep up; I'd get the gist of what he said and then fix it later if I needed to. She winked at me.

This was his letter:

> Dear Mom,
>   I'm doing just swell, except for the fact that my back still hurts like the devil. I intend to stay right here on my stomach until I feel like doing otherwise. Mrs. Nutter checked in this morning and I told her the same. But why tell you? I know you've heard by now, and visiting hours Sunday afternoon will find you or Dad here with the usual lecture. Since so much seems

to be going on behind, pardon me, my back, why don't you slip word to Dr. Nutter to give me something for the pain? Every time I move, I feel like the stitches are ripping out.

Now for some big news. Guess who's writing this letter for me? Charlie Kate Birch's granddaughter. And Dr. Birch herself is sitting right here. She seems to be very mean. You two would really get along swell. Her granddaughter doesn't appear to be that mean, though she did sit here and stare a hole through me when I had my eyes closed. You know how you can tell somebody's looking at you when your eyes are closed.

I'll sign off now. Don't forget when Dr. Nutter and you have your little daily chat to tell him I'm dying of pain. Nobody's listening to me. I truly feel like I'm in one of those nightmares where you think you're talking and you're only moving your mouth. There'd be nothing better than a little morphine right now. And some oatmeal cookies. If Esther's back from her honeymoon, how about asking her to make some and send them by you or Dad on Sunday?

Oh, you did a swell job beating up on the do-nothing legislature in this morning's column. Pretty soon you'll have to hire armed guards to take you to the grocery store.

Your son,
Tom

My grandmother told him this was satisfactory. Then she stood up and checked his back. She ran her finger along the stitches, and when he asked what she thought about his souvenir from the Pacific, she said, "By God, they certainly mangled you."

He said the Japanese had given him just a small dose, but it did evermore hurt.

She said, "I meant the surgeon. I could've done a better job with a Singer sewing needle and knitting yarn. And furthermore, they let a blind person shave you. You don't need morphine, but I'll have somebody bring you codeine. Then I want you up. You won't have an excuse to luxuriate."

He thanked her, and then asked if he could speak with me privately.

I believed he wanted to say something about her, maybe arrange a surprise meeting for his mother. My grandmother told him she wasn't a fan of privacy. She said, "I despise not knowing what people say."

He pushed himself up on his elbows again and said, "Well, I was going to ask your granddaughter if I could call her sometime."

I managed to say that would be fine, and my grandmother added, "Anytime before ten o'clock. Anybody calls our house after ten, I think somebody's dead in a ditch. We're in the phone book." She took my hand and tugged at me to leave, excusing us more graciously than I had expected. My cheeks were burning, and his were pulled back in a grin.

As we were leaving the ward, my grandmother stopped at the nurses' station and told someone to give the Hawkings boy some dry toast and orange juice and to call Dr. Nutter and request an order for codeine. Then she swung open the big metal door and held it for me. We walked to the Welfare and Recreation Office to sign out, and all the way down the hall she gave me instructions: "When you go on a date with that boy, mind your manners and tell him right up front you intend to go to college and *then* raise a family. And I'd also harp a bit on how expensive medical school is, and how much it costs to have somebody looking after the house and children, and things of that nature. Dwell on the high price of cooks. Don't nag him. Just line everything out."

After we signed out, she noticed a volunteer sheet for the hospital's holiday party, to be held the next evening. Without asking me, she wrote both our names in the punch table column. She told me I should take every chance that came along to see the young man. And then, on the way home, she spoke of him as if she knew everything about him. She said he had more assets than liabilities, and we'd have to stop him from saying "swell" so much, otherwise he'd drive her crazy. He was enormously intelligent, and he loved tussling with his mother. He wasn't impressed by his own good looks, and he was probably tired of giddy girls from the country club set. She continued, "Knowing what he does about me, he showed an admirable measure of audacity in asking in my presence to phone you, almost as much as it takes to read Thomas Mann in a military hospital. If any of these fellows caught on, they'd poison him. He thinks you have audacity to match. He was highly impressed with you sitting there staring at him."

Her reaction was so different from what it had been when my mother introduced Mr. Baines to her that I asked her why she hadn't yanked me away as she had my mother. She said, "That day I didn't know a thing about Mr. Baines other than that Sophia was slobbering over him, and you know what I've always thought of her judgment. But this Hawkings boy, I found out all I need to know about him, and I happen to think a little more highly of your judgment. He's not going to leave you alone. Not since Satan tackled Eve has somebody gone after a person as hard as he'll go after you. Am I correct?"

I told her I hoped she was, and because believing her was such a part of my training, I spent the rest of the day thrilled at the news that I'd marry this boy I'd just met, and go to medical school, and have a maid and children. I felt rushed to get all this under way, almost panicky. And then there was another thought: I felt sorry for all the people in the world who didn't have somebody around to predict their lives for them, all the girls who had no forewarning of what would become of them as women.

I asked whether Tom was ignorant of all this. Did she think he had any idea I might be more than some girl he felt like calling on the phone?

"He has a glimpse of it," she said. "He can't see everything, but he can see enough. I bet you the phone rings tonight. He wants to see the rest. Part of the fun will be showing it all to him." Then she jabbed me on the arm and said, "Ask him what he thinks of Mr. Faulkner. I'll hide and listen."

That evening I typed Tom's letter to his mother, making no changes. My grandmother included a note for her, stating her opinion about the ragged stitching and also that she had advised he be given codeine. She closed by saying, "I imagine we'll be meeting shortly."

But the next letter, the one from the Mississippi boy to his mother, was a complete fabrication. I told her that he appreciated the letters from the parishioners and that the crucifix over his bed meant the world to him. I enclosed the previous Sunday's comic strips with the letter, excluding *Little Orphan Annie.* The same thing could've happened as had happened with the Lumberton boy, but I did it anyway. She was as real to me, and as sad, as the mother I'd imagined sitting and crying on the cowboy-and-Indian bedspread. I could see her in her house in Jackson: She was a large woman. Her ankles tended to swell in the hot months. She dyed her hair. She was a maniac when it came to defending the Catholic Church and her family. I imagined the day her son would go home to her. She'd see him walking up the sidewalk, and she'd fall all over herself getting out the door to run and knock him down with kisses. She would scream and cry and blow her nose with a gaudy handkerchief and drag him inside the house and encourage him to have a big slice of day-old pound cake she had bought in honor of his return.

There would be much crying and nose-blowing, and then she would say something like, "Let's go over by the Bucket of Blood and show you off to your old daddy." They'd go and sit at the bar, and the father would ignore his yelling barmaids while he poured one drink for his son and two for himself, toasting the boy's exaggerated role in nipping the

Nips, slurring bawdy jokes that had enjoyed circulation when he was (probably) a private in the First War and which didn't seem that funny anymore. But all the people in the saloon would laugh because they would be either drunk enough to laugh at anything or sober enough to know that as long as the father of this returned sailor was merry, they could drink for free.

The father and mother and their son would hold each other up when they staggered home at daybreak. They'd drink chickory all morning, visit their neighbors all afternoon, and head back to the Bucket of Blood that night. I imagined that one of those horsehair Jesuses hung in every room of their house, grinning down on them at all times.

The phone rang at ten o'clock, just a few minutes after my grandmother had gone to bed. When I congratulated Tom for being up on his feet, he said he'd stunned the ward by getting out of bed to use the phone. "I credit my rise to your grandmother and the painkillers," he said. "Tell her the pills are doing a swell job." I liked that he was addicted to this word in spite of his education and taste in good literature. He asked when I was coming back to see him. He had the uncontrollable urge to dictate many letters. I told him I'd be there for the holiday party, pouring punch. He said it again. "That's just swell!" We ended the conversation by promising to keep our eyes open for each other.

MY GRANDMOTHER told me to wait to tell my mother I'd met someone who'd caught my eye. She said, "Tell her and you'll kick yourself. Wait awhile. Wait until she calms down." Why was my mother agitated? She was overly preoccupied with whether or not Mr. Baines would give her an engagement ring for Christmas, and constant thoughts of this had ground her nerves down to the quick. It was as if she were walking about our house snarling, "How about the two of you leave me alone so I can worry in peace?" I knew even without being told that after the matter was settled, after he had proposed on Christmas, I could tell her a young man had finally shown more than an academic interest in me and that I intended to show him the same. Mr. Baines had all but bought radio time and billboard space announcing his intentions, but my mother still had enough insecurity left over from her marriage to my father to cause her to pace about, calculating the odds of a happy ending, sniping at my grandmother and me if we chewed and swallowed too loudly.

The evening of the hospital party, Mr. Baines took my mother to the YMCA to hear a program of Filipino Christmas music. Who would've thought there was such a thing? After they left the house, I was eager to go ahead to the hospital, but my grandmother made me stay home with her until a special homefront broadcast of *Command Performance* was over. She had been excited about it since she had read the announcement on the entertainment page of the paper that morning. It promised a "can't-miss, won't-miss performance by Benny Goodman and a star-studded cast." She never missed an opportunity to hear Benny Goodman. I remember sitting by the radio with my coat and gloves on, waiting for her to say she'd heard enough to please her, but she didn't. All she said was, "Don't worry. He'll be there, and he'll not go anywhere. It's good to make him wait a little." We listened to the whole program. It was by far the best time I'd ever seen my grandmother have listening to the radio. Benny Goodman played all his hits. Nelson Eddy sang "Ah! Sweet Mystery of Life." Johnny Mercer sang "Deep in the Heart of Texas" for what seemed like fifteen minutes, and Hazel Scott played the "Minute Waltz" through the regular way once and then announced, "Now I'm going to break it down." It was eight o'clock when my grandmother let us leave.

By the time we reached the hospital, the party was going at full tilt. Louise Nutter greeted us very warmly and introduced us around to the doctors and their wives who had

stopped by. Very nonchalantly, I asked her how the Hawkings boy was doing. She told me he was much better and
would surely put in an appearance, as he had been caught
earlier that day bribing an orderly to have the already over-
worked hospital laundry press his dress blues for the occasion. She added, "That's just like him. I know a few nurses
who'll be relieved the day that one walks out of here." I
gathered that she believed his bribing the laundry was re-
flective of his pushy nature.

All the doctors seemed thrilled to see my grandmother,
more or less lining up to talk to her. I didn't see Tom
anywhere, but as I listened to my grandmother's conversa-
tions, my eyes roamed about the room. One surgeon engaged her in a long discussion about Sister Kenny. This
woman was an Australian nurse, later made famous by Rosa-
lind Russell, who revolutionized the treatment of infantile
paralysis. My grandmother told the surgeon that she'd been
performing the therapy for years. She described her
method: Instead of immobilizing a patient's legs, she'd wrap
them in hot blankets and flex the feet, and thus the leg
muscles, for intervals of five minutes, for an hour a day or
for as long as the patient could stand it. The surgeon asked
how it worked for her. She told him it wasn't the miracle it
was now trumped up to be, but it did make her patients
more comfortable. He said he was amazed she had strayed
from orthodox practice on her own authority. I could tell
she was pleased with herself. She didn't tell him anything
like, "Oh, but I specialize in the unorthodox" or "I am a
great believer in variations on a routine." She didn't respond

in any way that would've been thoroughly appropriate and justified. She merely smiled and, in the most cordial way, invited herself into his operating room. She wanted to see some new method of cauterization she'd read about. He told her she was welcome anytime.

Then he brought up the subject of "the operating fool," a California man who had recently been arrested for operating on people without a license. My grandmother said, "If you intend the story of his capture as a moral lesson to me, you can save your breath." He started to tell her he had mentioned the story only because it was humorous, but he stopped when she began talking over him, listing her kitchen table surgeries, from the sawmill worker and the red thread on through five procedures for major lacerations, several amputations of toes and fingers, and one failed attempt at reattaching a finger lopped off by a bread knife. This attempt she blamed on the knife: "It was the serrated edge. That's why I couldn't do it." The surgeon gently told her that reattaching appendages was beyond medical science. She said, "It might be, but I still think I could've done it had the woman been using a smooth-edge. I know I could have." The surgeon had by then heard enough to let her have her way.

I excused myself to pour punch. I told my grandmother I'd be back when my shift was up. It seemed endless. A clot of young men started hanging about the refreshment table. They recognized me from having seen me on their wards, reading and writing letters, but unlike the young men I'd helped with letters, these five seemed intent on, as was said

at the time, making me. If they weren't telling me a sob story
they were handing me a line. One held a bandaged hand up
in front of my face and asked, "Know how this happened?"
I remember I had to pull my head back to keep the hand
from jabbing me in the nose. I said I was sorry but I didn't
know how he'd been hurt. "Guess. Just take a guess," he
said. From the smell on him, I suspected he had liquor
hidden somewhere and this would make him overbearing
and relentless. I was right. He wouldn't let go. I kept saying
I had no idea how he'd gotten hurt, although my instinct was
that he'd been wounded not in a battle but in a bawdy-
house brawl. His chums were saying things like, "Yeah,
girlie. Take a shot at it." This teasing persisted even as I was
pouring punch for people who came up to the table. These
people stared at us, but they would give me no relief. I finally
said, "Listen, I'm really busy. How about you all find somebody else to quiz, okay?"

This made things worse. One of them said I was cute
when I was mad. I threatened to have one of the military
policemen who was guarding the fire exits arrest him. The
one with the bad hand said, "For what? Trying to get to
know you? You sure are a cold one, girlie." They were of the
unsavory sort who whipped up the zoot suit riots, much
rougher characters than the hoodlums I'd always been so
easily able to disperse in the school parking lot. I was used
to saying, "Okay, guys, let's pick up those bottles and butts
and move along," and having boys twice my size nod, bend
over, pick up their litter, and throw it in a trashcan. I hadn't
changed since those days.

I like to think I had a demure way about me and didn't appear to be fodder for this gang. But for all these fellows knew, I could've been secretly easy, and all they had to do was make me admit what I *really* wanted. I could've been one of those homefront girls they'd been hearing about who had grown so lonesome for a man that they would toss all morals aside and hop in the backseat. I could've been listening to too much Frank Sinatra, longing for romance, something trite like that. I could've been without my boyfriend for six months, and consequently so full of untapped passion that I was ready to explode. Or I could've been another Arlene, mindlessly ranging around, sampling whatever was handy.

I imagined Tom appearing, chivalrous and larger than life in his dress blues, telling these guys to go crawl back under their rocks, but he was nowhere to be seen. I remember glaring at my grandmother's back as she held forth to her string of doctors, hoping I could will her to turn around and see me. She would've come over screaming and offered to castrate all five of them. But she wouldn't turn around. Mrs. Nutter finally saw my plight and came over with an officer. He called the five by name and stripped them of radio, visiting, and general dayroom and recreational privileges for the next week. They responded with a sharp salute and moved away from the table, still in that one clot. Mrs. Nutter apologized, relieved me of the rest of my shift, and reminded me to tell my grandmother when hers started.

My grandmother had just left the group of people she had accumulated around her, and had taken a seat in a row of chairs set up against the wall. This put her in the middle of all the girls who had come that evening in hopes of finding a lonely single fellow and his allotment check. They had that look about them. Girls like these, who showed up at dances, went in carloads to the coast to wave troop ships off, and hung about downtown outside the Enlisted Men's Recreation Room, were called "Allotment Annies." This hospital group made as captive an audience as they were likely to find anywhere. Although the public was trained to spot such girls, the ones who had come to the hospital party didn't seem to be suffering from their shameful reputation. Patients who could get around well enough to dance picked them off the wall, danced and chatted, and then delivered them back to wait for the next partner. The girls rotated in and out of their chairs so fast that I doubt the seats had time to get cold.

There was, or at least I hoped there was, a great visible distinction between these girls and me. I had on white gloves. They had bare hands. My hat had been made in Washington. Their hats appeared to be from Woolworth's. I had on stockings. Most of these girls were wearing Liquid Stocking, and perspiration from all their dancing had streaked color down the back of their calves. I remember their purses especially: I was sure that for whatever was in them, they could've been left at home. If the girls had been asked to dump out the contents of their purses in the middle of the floor, think of everything that would've spilled out: nickels and pennies, hard candy, dime-store lipstick, rouge, and nail polish, compacts, rabbit's feet, loose stale cigarettes, and butts they'd picked out of their fathers' ashtrays and straightened out. I thought of how the young men who had harassed me could've saved themselves valuable wolfing time had they gravitated first to this crowd. And then I saw them, down at the far end of the row, working on a few of these girls, showing that fellow's bandaged hand around. I wondered whether they were telling them about the stick-in-the-mud they'd run into over by the punch bowl.

I had to ask several girls to move down the row to open up a seat by my grandmother. Sitting there in the middle of them, she looked like a chaperone at a wayward girls' school outing. When I sat down, she leaned over and said to me, "Look at this bunch. They're wound up like nymphs at carnival time." They were. They were all patting their feet to the music, snapping their fingers, waxing that horrible clove chewing gum that I had thought to be rationed. They seemed to have found a bottomless supply. As I sat there by them, I wondered how many of their fathers knew their daughters were out of the house. I had read accounts of parents in port towns locking their daughters inside when troop ships came in and then finding their daughters gone anyway, having pried open windows and shimmied down drain pipes. The girl beside me was sixteen going on twenty-two, all dolled up in an ill-fitting dress and that cheap makeup that grows orange with time. Her nails were chewed so low that her fingertips looked inflamed, and she kept trying secretly to smooth her makeup down onto her neck. I wondered whether she had pried nails out of her bedroom window, held her purse in her teeth, and let herself down the side of her house.

My grandmother was due to say something directly to the girls. She was due to tell the one beside her to go to the bathroom and wash that brown mess off her legs. She didn't. I asked her how she felt about all this, all these wound-up girls trotting on and off the floor like dime-dancers. She told me it was no different from the First War. "Everybody's morals went to hell," she said. "You couldn't go to a Grange party without seeing a girl doing a shake-down dance, showing her linen. And then two years later, orphanages were stacked to the roof." She looked around the room and pointed out several couples who she said should've proceeded directly to the parking lot. "They could skip all the dancing and go climb in the car. For the duration of the war, sex is here to stay."

Dr. Nutter came over and asked if he could get us anything. My grandmother said he could not, but he could tell her why he allowed entry to all these strumpets. She said, "It compromises the dignity of this hospital." He said he knew but he couldn't help it. The party was open to the public, and no harm was being done. She begged to differ, and then they entered a lengthy discussion on wartime morale and morals. My grandmother glanced at me, noticed my distracted state, and told me not to worry. She said, "He'll be here." So I sat there and waited, looking at the girls all around me, trying as best as I could not to make eye contact. Not only were they fast, they were tough, the kind of girls who might form a pack, follow me to the bathroom, and ask point-blank, "So, prissy, what do you think you're looking at?"

I was busy looking at the girl with the chewed nails out

of the corner of my eye, pretending to listen to my grandmother and Dr. Nutter, when a voice said, "Boy, you sure
look bored."

It was Tom, standing in front of my chair. He looked
different, even better, upright and fully clothed. I told him
hello, and no, I wasn't bored, just a little tired. He told me
he would have come sooner if he'd not had to wait forever
for his uniform to get back from the laundry.

He said, "Just a minute," and then spoke to the girl next
to me. She was biting one of her nails so furiously that she
seemed intent on chewing off her hand to the wrist. He
asked her to move so he could sit down.

She obeyed him and slid over, still chewing. She didn't
stare at him the way I had the first time I met him. She
didn't try to make him. For all the loosening of morals going
on that night, this girl was not loosening the social rule that
forbade a poor southside girl with orange makeup and mangled, gloveless hands to flirt with somebody her mother
might wait on at City Grill or her father might mop up after
at a fraternity house.

When Tom sat down, Dr. Nutter greeted him and said he
looked in fine shape. My grandmother said, "Yes, you give
somebody a little of what they're begging for, and they might
start to come around. You can't treat these boys all the
same." Dr. Nutter could feel an embarrassing lecture on
varying pain thresholds coming his way, so he excused himself. My grandmother told us she'd rather talk to us anyway.
She settled herself in for our conversation.

Tom told her how much better his back felt, and then

stared off as if he didn't know what else to say. He squinted, trying to think of something.

My grandmother saw what was happening to him and offered to help. "Why don't you ask her to dance?" she said.

His ears turned red, and then he asked me. I told him I'd like nothing better. I hoped his lead was strong enough for me to follow without giving away the fact that I had absolutely no idea what I was doing. My grandmother told me to leave my scarf on my chair and my gloves on his, lest a couple of strumpets decided to steal our seats when she wasn't looking.

He danced with assurance, and the slightly rigid manner with which he held his back gave his movements an air of dignity one didn't usually see on a wartime dance floor. I figured he must have been given an extra dose of codeine that evening, the way he danced without grimacing the way he'd done when he propped himself up on his elbows. He even carried me through on a couple of sane jitterbugs, touching the small of my back and steering me out of the way of partners throwing each other around with such violent force that I wondered that their arms weren't being yanked out of the sockets. Jitterbugging had just been outlawed on the Duke campus, not so much for moral reasons as because of the numbers of students landing in the infirmary with dislocated shoulders. The floor was so packed that when one couple moved, we all moved. Half of the young men had on uniforms, and the other half had on pajamas and green hospital robes. One hung on a pair of crutches, like a scarecrow, while his partner shook everything she had in front of him, reaching out to grab his hand every now and then to whip herself around. She appeared to be double-jointed.

Between numbers Tom pointed to the orchestra, a thrown-together group of 4-F musicians from the North Carolina Symphony, and told me the pianist was his sister. She had finished her exams early, and the minute she was home she was recruited to play with this group. He waved at her, and she gave him an okay sign with her fingers. I wondered what she had heard about me. I wondered whether he'd told her I was swell. Next we danced to the song my grandmother most despised. When I heard the opening strains of "White Christmas," I looked at her to say, "Yes, I know you hate it, but I'm going to stay put. If you want me off the dance floor, you'll have to drag me." She made a face to show me how revolted she was, and then got up to start her shift at the punch bowl. Tom held me so close that I could separate all the odors on his skin, his soap and shaving cream and after-shave and his own scent, that sort of man's scent that was foreign to me.

When the song was over, and he asked whether I'd like to keep going or sit down, I said, "Keep going. By all means." Before the next song started, he pulled me to the edge of the stage and whistled his sister over to us. She smiled very sweetly at me and leaned down so he could whisper in her ear. Then she walked away and spoke to the orchestra leader. The next two songs were "I'll Be Seeing You" and "You Made Me Love You." He told me they were the only slow numbers he could think of. He had noticed how self-conscious I was fast-dancing, and had wanted me to feel more at ease. I thought, If it keeps on like this, how did I ever rate to be so lucky?

While we were dancing, he asked about my life. I gave him a slim history, and when he asked why I wasn't in college, I told him the truth: I hadn't been able to leave home. He said, "Everybody's got to do it sometime," and then pressed his fingers, I could feel all five, into my back and changed the subject to symbols in *The Magic Mountain.* A young woman has never learned so much on a dance floor.

We danced until my grandmother's shift was over. She looked ready to leave, and she busied herself with her coat and gloves to give me time to say good night. It must have taken everything she had for her not to rush up and ask him when, exactly, he planned to see me again. I told him how grand a time I'd had. I wanted to ask him whether he realized by now how thoroughly inevitable we were, but I asked him instead when he thought he'd be discharged from the hospital. He said he had two more days there. His medical evaluation had come through that morning, and because some shrapnel was lodged too close to his spine, he wasn't being sent back into active duty. He was going to spend the next three weeks in Asheville, at the Grove Park Inn, where some German prisoners, all officers, had just been taken. He would be replacing the translator, who was taking a long holiday leave. He said, "The dogfaces have Christmas leave canceled, and this guy takes off more than Mr. Roosevelt." I asked how he'd become so proficient in German, and he told me he had studied languages at Washington and Lee. After Christmas, he would come back to Raleigh and work in the recruitment center. I was still trying to process the part about his studying languages, when he asked what my plans were. I told him the truth. I was going to sit around the house and read, plot troop movements, write hospital letters, and hope somebody broke a leg or something so my grandmother and I would have something exciting to do.

This is what he said to me: "You left out writing me."

Wasn't that something for him to say?

THE NEXT DAY during break-
fast, a courier brought a letter to me:

Dear Margaret,
   I've just talked to you on the phone. You sounded
tired. Better get some rest, because when I get back
from Asheville I have plans for you. I'll go ahead and
say what they are, so you'll have plenty of time to shop.
First, how would you like to go with me to my sister's
recital at Peace College on the 28th? Afterward, my
parents are giving a party. I hesitate to ask this because
it may sound like I'm using you to get to your grandmother, but if she could come along, that'd be swell.
I suspect my mother's giving the party just to meet her
anyway. But she can't go to the next thing, the Sphinx
Club's New Year's Eve Party. And then the next day
there's the New Year's Day party at Carolina Country
Club. This is when all my parents' friends eat black-

eyed peas and talk about how broke they used to be. Somebody who knows Kay Kyser actually talked him into playing. I know by now you're probably wondering why I don't already have a date so close to these events. I'll tell you why. I wasn't going to go to any of them. Not because of my back. I just wasn't in the mood. I was going to spend the time, as your grandmother puts it, lazing off. Go ahead and mark all these dates down, okay?

I'll call before I leave, and see how they suit you. By the way, my dad owns Serotta's Dress Shop. Don't let me insult you by sounding cheap, but if you'll let me call the manager, you can get a huge discount on anything you'd like. Same thing with office supplies and shoes. Sometimes I think Dad bought up all those stores because Mom hates paying retail and has yet to adjust to rationing. And one more thing. The courier who brought this letter to you works for my dad. Somehow he fixed the boy up with a C card. He drives all over everywhere doing all sorts of minor errands for my folks. If you need anything picked up or delivered, just call Worthwhile Office Supplies and ask for Bobby. See how having me around might come in handy?

A nurse is writing this for me. She seems to be running out of steam, so I'll close. The splint comes off tomorrow, and the next day I'll leave for Asheville. I've requested the room Fitzgerald stayed in when he was visiting Zelda, but I was told that twenty college boys were already lined up to take a turn sleeping a night in it.

I forgot to tell you that my job also involves censor-

ing letters. I'll pass along anything juicy the Germans
tell the Fräuleins back home. Just kidding.

Best wishes,
Tom Hawkings III

I read the letter through several times and then asked my
grandmother if she wanted to read it. She did, and as she
folded it back into the envelope, she said, "This is good. Go
to everything. Do something about your hair. Practice dancing with the doorknob. Have a letter waiting for him when
he gets to Asheville."

I asked her if she'd go to the recital and his parents' party.
She said she would, and then she told me to put the letter
away and say nothing of it to my mother, as she was still
suffering a prolonged period of acute worry and did not
need the added distraction. I knew my mother couldn't talk
me out of this, but my grandmother seemed unwilling to
listen to her try. Once again, my loyalties were divided, and
I followed my grandmother's advice because of her lifelong
winning streak. She said, "Sophia's wearing her leg out
putting her best foot forward for Richard. I've never seen
her want something so badly."

I suggested that one of us talk to Mr. Baines. Maybe he
could go ahead and ask her to marry him. My grandmother
said we could not. He had his idea of what would be perfect,
and down the road he might start to resent my mother's
inability to wait. My grandmother said, "When a marriage
goes sour, two things start to happen. You can't look at the
other person chew and so you stare at your plate all through

dinner, and you can't sleep at night for harboring thoughts of how the one lying beside you spoiled something you wanted. Things go downhill fast when you can't eat and sleep together, which are what married people are supposed to enjoy doing the most. Look at how that very thing ate at Sophia. How many times has she cried over the yellow shoes and raw-onion odor?" She concluded that Mr. Baines had shown he knew what was best for my mother, and if he wanted to propose on Christmas or New Year's, my mother would have to bear the strain of waiting. I didn't remind my grandmother of her own inability to wait, all the times she had squirmed and huffed through the cartoons before the feature presentation, all the times she had stood in ration lines with me and shouted, "What's the holdup?"

I wrote Tom back that afternoon. I accepted all the invitations, although I did decline his kind offer of discounts and free courier service. When he called that evening, I sat on a tall wooden stool and told him, I felt sure, everything I had ever known. He was leaving early the next morning for Asheville. There was no way I could get to the hospital in time to see him.

Later, when I got there and started my shift, I saw that his bed had been taken by a tow-headed boy whose right leg was packed in sandbags from hip to toe. His right arm was amputated at the elbow. I wasn't assigned to him, but I asked if I could help with correspondence anyway. I read a letter his sister had sent, and he dictated one to her in return. There was nothing incredible or even mildly interesting about either.

It took just a few minutes with the Mississippi boy to cheer me up. He accomplished this by telling me about the long-distance call his mother had made to him since our last visit. He had asked her about William Faulkner, and he was anxious to tell me her final word on him. He said, "Margaret, I hate to tell you, but Mama says Mr. Faulkner is a big liar and everybody in Mississippi knows it. Maybe you ought to give a little thought to this." He seemed genuinely concerned about the state of my soul. When I met my grandmother for lunch in the cafeteria, I told her right away that Mr. Faulkner had just been revealed as a big liar. She laughed and said, "Yes, and if he told simpler lies, he'd make a better living."

When we got home, we saw that my mother had trimmed the tree by herself. She was sitting on the floor putting the tops back on empty ornament boxes. My grandmother asked whether she had left anything for us to do. She said she had not, and if we looked on the desk, we would see that she had finished writing the Christmas cards as well. Although she didn't say this, it was clear to me that she had used these chores as a way of burning up nervous energy. My grandmother walked straight to the tree and started moving ornaments around, saying how this one had always been closer to the top and this one closer to the bottom. My mother stood watching with her hands on her hips. She looked as if she wished she had the nerve to shout out loud, "You've always got to have something to do, don't you? And if you can't see it, you'll invent it, won't you? Everything from organizing people's lives to saving them to moving crystal icicles around on a Christmas tree." After the ornaments were in their new places, my grandmother pronounced the tree finished, and then she sat down with a book. She was caught up for the day. I sat by her and read and waited.

We waited for the mailman, for *Are You a Missing Heir?* and *Dr. I.Q.*, for Edward R. Murrow, Christmas, promised snow, and all the rest of the things I felt were coming in my life. Two weeks before, I hadn't known what I wanted my life to look like, but now I knew. That's why there was no fear when I stepped off into the middle of it.

I wrote letters to Asheville daily, sending them special delivery, and received two, sometimes three, from Tom each day. I learned many things about him. He loved having a full tank of gas, having his ears cleaned out, having a good haircut. He loved the way it felt when the barber brushed talcum powder on the back of his neck. It was plain that he wouldn't be a lifetime, swinging date. He was a lean horse for a long race. He and I went about life at the same tempo.

I always let my grandmother read a draft of my letters before they went out. She made corrections and detailed suggestions in the margins and on the back of the letters. She'd say, "Tell about the blimp we saw yesterday. Tell him how low it passed, how it made all the dogs howl." Or, "Tell him you're a fast study and could learn poker if he was willing to teach you." Or, "Ask if he's planning to go by the Wolfe boardinghouse. Tell him you thought *Of Time and the River* was long-winded, overwrought, and not to be believed." I incorporated many of her suggestions and was always pleased with the results, but then I made my own additions, things she never saw. I never let her see how I moved from signing the letters "Your friend" to "Sincerely" to "Yours truly" to simply "Yours." I let her read all his letters to me except the last two. In these, he said he had looked for me all his life. He said it over and over. Although she had told me this would happen, I couldn't let her see the direct evidence that it had.

This was the first time in my life I had hidden anything from her. It was the first time I had had an emotion so thoroughly my own that I felt the need to guard it from her view. She did see the evidence of these last letters on my face, indirectly, in the way I couldn't keep my thoughts straight, in the way I ruined a copper kettle, boiling it dry, and then went to the shed to get firewood in thirty-degree weather, barefooted. I bleached a green blouse and consistently answered calls for other members of our party line. I did something equally mindless each time I finished reading one of Tom's letters, and as a result I had to walk about the house conscious of every move I made, trying to appear normal. My mother, as concerned as she was about her own self, noticed my behavior. One day she said, "You're not yourself. What's distracted you?" "Oh, just this and that," I told her. "So much seems to be going on these days." I tried to make my concerns sound too numerous to list. She kept on. "You look like you get no sleep. You whisper to your grandmother incessantly. Is it the schools? Are you two in cahoots again over schools?" I tried to throw her off. I told her, if she had to know, we were. She rushed out of the room and told my grandmother that she was perfectly capable of advising me about when and where to go. She said, "You have her addled." My grandmother accepted full responsibility for my state, saying, "Sophia, you can blame it all on me. I'm used to it. I'll listen to anything you have to say." She gave my mother nothing to push against, and consequently my mother did not push. She put on her coat and went to the movies.

I wasn't lying when I said so much was going on. That December of 1942 was without parallel. Eddie Rickenbacker told the story of being adrift for twenty-three days, how a sea gull landed on his head and answered his incessant prayers for food. Rommel started his retreat into Tunisia. The Russians crossed the Volga and attacked the Germans. My mother and grandmother and I were watching *White Cargo,* when the projectionist interrupted the film to run the newsreel that showed the Russians' advance. The theater erupted in an uproar. I will never forget the first scene of the movie that appeared after the newsreel was over. It was Hedy Lamarr in that black strapless jungle dress, begging Walter Pidgeon to beat her. My grandmother was disgusted. She left her seat, after whispering to me that she was going to walk down to City News and Candy to tell her friends about the Russians. A couple of the men there had been encamped in the first American position established on the other side of the Hindenburg Line, in 1918. They were always highly interested in war news, but even though they were surrounded by newspapers, the only news they learned was what people brought to the store and told them. There was no radio, as the owner of the place said he didn't believe in noise.

When my mother and I picked my grandmother up after the movie, she reeked of cigarette smoke and gin. She fell asleep on the couch before supper.

The next morning we read that Churchill had called Mussolini a hyena, and Mussolini called him one back; their exchange inspired my grandmother to call my mother a hyena for the next three days. We read that the fattest lady in the world, whom my grandmother and I had paid a nickel apiece to see at the October state fair, had died in Florida; she had been as large as the overstuffed mohair chair in our living room. That a local man had been shot by his wife after dealing her a bad bridge hand. That the state legislature had passed a sanitation law prohibiting witnesses in court trials from kissing the Bible; Tom's mother had a field day with this in her column. That the city of Charlotte had become so distressed by Charles Lindbergh's America First activities that on December 7 the city council changed the name of Lindbergh Avenue to something else.

Just when December seemed to be so full of news that it was ready to topple over into the new year, a woman of apparent means and sophistication arrived in Raleigh, on the morning of Christmas Eve. Within hours everybody in town knew about her, all her details. She was wearing a red gabardine wool suit of a European cut with a white fox collar, and a red fedora with white satin trim. Her legs were so slender and so long they seemed to proceed right up through her red suit to her throat. And she was blonde. It looked to be her natural color.

Late in the afternoon of Christmas Eve, I answered a call from the desk clerk at the Sir Walter Hotel. She had previously worked at the county courthouse and had supplied my grandmother with birth records and addresses for twenty years. That was as much as she knew us. Her reasons for phoning were of that slightly salacious nature that compels some women to revel in other women's difficulties with men. She whispered to me—which made no sense at all, as I know she broadcast the news to everybody who walked through the hotel lobby. She told me that a woman calling herself Mrs. Richard Baines had checked in and had booked a room for two weeks. Then she described the woman's clothing as if she were narrating a fashion show, commenting on the elegance of her gait, her finishing-school voice. The woman was all class, collar to cuff. She asked what my mother would say.

I told her I didn't know, and then I thanked her for calling. Also, I told her I was sure she'd keep this to herself, which was tantamount to telling the Nile not to rise.

Mr. Baines and his mother were due to arrive in thirty minutes. We were planning to have eggnog and beignets. My mother and grandmother were in the guest bedroom wrapping presents. I walked in without knocking. On the bed were all my Santa Claus presents, boxed and wrapped, ready for my mother to place underneath the tree at daybreak. As blunt an attitude as they both had about the world and its fantasies, they still insisted that I get up on Christmas morning and act surprised to see that Santa Claus had come. I knew what was in the boxes: a chenille robe, the latest Ellen Glasgow and Katherine Anne Porter novels, a copy of *Saturday Review of Literature,* which meant I was being given a year's subscription, and a small velvet box that I believed contained the mother-of-pearl earrings I had lingered over in the Neiman-Marcus catalogue.

I worried that the thirty minutes before Mr. Baines's arrival would be chewed up by my inability to get to the point. He would get there before I told my news, and he would announce it himself. He would say, "My ex-wife is in town. We're planning to see each other while she's here, and there's no saying what might happen, and for that I am truly sorry." My father's yellow wedding shoes and infidelities would look like practice rounds for that announcement. I wasn't sure my mother could recover.

They wanted to know what was wrong. Had I seen the afternoon paper? Was somebody from my class on the casualty list? I must've looked terrible.

I said, "Well, a lady got to town a little while ago, this morning to be precise, and she has this, well, sort of this *name.*"

My grandmother told me to get myself together and tell them, in simple, direct English, what was going on. I was to tell the story when I could do so without the help of "well," "and ah," "um," and "you know." I said, "Okay. There's a lady who's calling herself Mrs. Richard Baines. She's staying at the Sir Walter for two weeks. It may not be anything, but I thought you ought to know."

My mother didn't deny this could be true. Neither did my grandmother. They didn't team up against me and say that I had imagined the conversation or that the clerk had imagined the vision or misunderstood the name. Women with less experience in the areas of loneliness, abandonment, betrayal, and other furious pursuits might have thought first: "Oh, that can't be right." But not these two. They believed the worst, I suppose, as a means of self-protection. My mother's face told me this. Within seconds, she looked as if someone's big hand had started at her forehead and moved down over her face, pulling her features, smearing misery over her as it went. Something inside her seemed to have shut off. She couldn't speak. If she had tried, I think, she would've grunted the way children do when they fall off high swings and get the wind knocked out of them. My grandmother began spitting out questions to which I had no answer, and got irritated when I didn't know such things as where the woman had come from, why she had come, whether or why Mr. Baines invited her, and why, after two years, she was still flagging his name around. My grandmother believed that last fact to be highly revealing about the nature of the woman's visit. When it became clear that I was ignorant on each point, she said I was no good, no good at all, if that was the only information I had. She strode toward the kitchen to phone the hotel clerk, saying, "I'm determined to know everything."

The call was never made. She heard Mr. Baines's car as

she was dialing the hotel number. I was still in the guest room with my mother. The two of us stood very quietly. I had the feeling I was behind a thick, sound wall, waiting for the explosion, like a British woman huddled under a stout table, waiting. Mr. Baines opened the back door, and I started to ask my mother if she wanted me to go out there with her.

She said, "Shh. Mother's got him."

If he had known who and what lay in wait for him, he would've driven past our house, slowing just enough to toss our gifts in the yard without breaking anything. He called out, "Merry Christmas! Anybody home?" I heard him tell his mother to watch her step. He opened the door to the kitchen, and there stood my grandmother.

She said, "And a Merry Christmas to you and that other one you've got stuck up at the Sir Walter. Sit down and wait for me while I get your mother situated." Then she called out for me to help her.

I asked my mother if she was sure she shouldn't go in there with me. Her great dread had pooled around the corners of her mouth, showing deep creases I had never noticed. She said, "I told you, *Mother's* got him. Just go do what she says."

My grandmother was leading Mr. Baines's mother to the big mohair chair, the one that was the size of the side-show lady, and shouting in her ear, "Look here! We're going to drag a fern over by you. Enjoy yourself."

After my grandmother and I had scraped the floor pulling the planter across the room, Mrs. Baines frowned at the fern and then at me and said, "This isn't mine. Mine is pretty, very pretty. This one isn't mine." I could've been a nurse who'd brought her the wrong child to take home from the hospital. She kept on with how this wasn't hers, how hers was very pretty, actually, very, very pretty.

My grandmother said, "I *know* this isn't yours. Just pretend it is. Baby-sit it."

Mr. Baines was waiting for us at the kitchen door. He asked my grandmother what she had meant. Who was at the Sir Walter? He sounded innocent. In fact, he sounded so thoroughly blameless that I would've acquitted him at that moment. My grandmother, having a much dimmer view of human nature, pressed him.

She said, "You mean to tell me you don't know who just checked in at the hotel?"

He said he did not know, but he believed he was about to be told.

If my grandmother had had a whip, she'd have cracked it. She shouted out loud, "Sophia! Come tell him who's at the hotel!"

My mother was barely in the room before my grandmother said again, "Tell him, Sophia. Tell him who it is who's in town."

Mr. Baines looked at my mother in a pleading sort of way. She said, "Richard, your ex-wife's in town. She's planning to stay for two weeks."

He swore he didn't know.

My mother asked how he could not know. She started to cry, and I pulled out a chair for her and one for myself. He said it again. He had no idea.

216

My grandmother said she didn't believe him. A woman wouldn't show up uninvited on Christmas Eve, flagging her ex-husband's name around, carrying what must be two weeks' worth of luggage.

He said, "Well, yes she would. She's been having some problems lately."

My mother asked him how he knew, and he told us he had talked to her recently. She called him after she received news of her brother's death in Italy. "She was very blue," he said. "Her father died early in the year. Her mother died the year before. This is her first Christmas alone. She said she wanted to come to Raleigh and visit, just visit for a while. I told her that would be inappropriate, but she's always had her own ideas about what is and isn't appropriate. So she came."

I believe my mother thought he sounded a little too sorry for the woman. I certainly thought so. It worried me that all that compassion would get him into trouble. My mother laid her head on the table. She was struggling to cry without making noise, like a mad little girl who's been made to keep her head on her desk during recess. I rubbed her back a bit, and then did something I hadn't done since I was a child. I smelled of my fingertips. There was that same scent of baby powder that I used to smell on my hands as I lay in bed after I had rubbed her back at night. When I was first sent to school, I would only pretend to wash my hands in the morning, so I could then sit in the classroom and pretend to listen, with my fingers up in front of my nose. What a sight we must have made for Mr. Baines! My grandmother looking so murderous. Me sniffing my fingertips. He sat across the table from the three of us, squeezing his eyes together toward his nose the way men do when they're trying to fend off tears. He asked if he could talk to my mother alone.

My grandmother said, "There *is* no alone here."

He didn't argue about that. He said he'd just wanted to explain things. Maybe he should go to the hotel. Maybe he should call. He didn't know. He rattled on, explaining why he was having such difficulty explaining himself. My grandmother interrupted and said, "Just tell me this. Do you want Sophia or don't you?"

He said he did.

"Well, that settles that," she said. "You can't have two. Having two is against my rules. Start the car. I'll get my coat."

He asked where they were headed.

She said they were going to town. She was planning to sit in the car and wait for him to tell the woman she was going back where she belonged.

"But it's Christmas," he said. He couldn't let somebody down on Christmas. He pitied her. Didn't we feel sorry for somebody who showed up like that, still using her husband's name two years after their divorce?

My grandmother asked him if he realized how much gall it had taken for the woman to do this. She said, "Hell, I wouldn't even do that. Neither would Sophia."

Mr. Baines was careful not to sound plaintive when he asked again that the woman be left alone until Christmas had passed. He said he'd take her to dinner, and that was all, and if we were worried, we were welcome to come along.

My mother lifted her head. She said, "Richard, I've listened all I'm going to. I'll say this once: If you don't do it
to her on Christmas, I'll do it to you."

My grandmother stood up and said, "She's right. Go get
the car."

He asked if we had any idea how large a penalty would
be charged to change a train reservation. My grandmother
found her purse, made a check out to Seaboard Coast Line
and handed it to Mr. Baines, saying, "I didn't expect you to
pay for this. They'll take care of it at the front desk. That
ought to keep tongues wagging in town for six months or
more." She explained that she could run a woman out of
town on a rail on Christmas Eve, but she would reimburse
her for her trouble. Mr. Baines said he couldn't accept her
money. He'd created the mess, and he'd pay to clean it up.
My grandmother tore the check in two and tossed the pieces
in the trashcan, saying, "Good. Now, let's go." As she tied
her old nappy scarf under her chin, she said, "Sophia, I'll be
back in a little bit. Get yourself together while I'm gone."

Mr. Baines tried to touch my mother on the arm, but she
wouldn't let him. "Get rid of her," she said. "And don't you
ever do this to me again." She ran to her room and slammed
the door. We could hear her big, heaving cries.

So off my grandmother went, to sit alone in a dark car
parked in front of the Sir Walter. I wondered whether she
laughed to herself at how this hotel was now the place where
two generations of Birch women had taken hold of their
lives. I imagined her wondering whether someday I'd make

my own trip there. As she had predicted, Mr. Baines needed very little time to sort out his life. He was in the hotel for twenty minutes. Of all the things we knew or thought we had known about Mr. Baines, there was one singular truth: He was too much of a gentleman to let an old lady wait a long time in an automobile. He would correct his life in a hurry and rush back to my grandmother, apologizing all the way home that he was sorry to have kept her waiting. This certain fact of his gentlemanly nature thus came in very handy for us all.

Mr. Baines's mother and I listened to the radio while they were away. When I asked if I could get her anything, she said she wanted some cookies. She was very adamant about this. I told her we had none. She said, "How long am I supposed to be here?" I told her I wasn't sure. She told me that if I intended for her to stay, I'd find some cookies. I remember staring at the Pasquotank mantel clock, hoping Mr. Baines and my grandmother would return in a hurry. When they did, Mr. Baines went directly to my mother's room. I heard her door open to let him in, and that was all I heard for a time.

My grandmother sat down and engaged Mrs. Baines in conversation about past Christmases. The old woman started cataloguing every gift she had ever gotten or given—a true feat for someone whose life had been reduced to watering ferns and asking her son to tell her, one more time, exactly what his name was. She didn't mention what had seemed to be an immoderate desire for cookies. She was describing a fleur-de-lis pin her husband had given her in 1920 when we heard my mother and Mr. Baines coming down the hall. He was carrying a suitcase. My mother was wearing a black tricorne hat and her sable jacket. She stopped in front of us and spoke with not a grain of emotion, the way she talked to my grandmother's patients when she explained exactly what was about to be done to a lacerated foot or an abscessed gum. She said, "Richard and I are driving to South Carolina tonight to get married. Then we're going to the Atlantis for a week. There's nothing to do at the beach in the winter, but we're going anyway."

My grandmother asked who had thought of this. Mr. Baines said they had decided together. He had planned to propose the next morning and then have the service sometime in the spring, but they had chosen to go ahead now.

I asked my mother how she felt about these plans. She knew I was asking her if this wasn't another version of the first one. How would she feel when the proprietor of one of those tacky chapels told her he didn't accept checks or ration coupons, cash only? And how would she feel when his wife walked out of the back room to witness the ceremony, wearing curlers in her hair, bedroom slippers, smelling of cheap toilet water that might call up the raw-onion odor?

My mother said, "I'm okay. This is what I want. I'd rather have it this way than wait. Don't worry about me. Just please look after Richard's mother until her nurse starts back to work." She wasn't smiling, but she looked happy. Her pleasure was solid, bone-deep, the sort that outlives perfect proposals and ceremonies. Mr. Baines wore this same look. I remember thinking how good it was that their faces matched.

His mother came up out of her fog and asked where

everybody was going. Mr. Baines squatted in front of her and calmly explained everything, and then said, "Remember when I asked if I could have the ring Dad gave you? Remember that?"

She spread the fingers of her left hand out and pointed to a large ring crusty with diamonds. She looked at it as though she were seeing it for the first time and asked, "This one?"

He said, "Yes, Mother, that one."

She pulled it off her finger and held it out to him, saying, "Don't lose it, or I'll flail you." He promised he would not.

My grandmother apologized that she couldn't donate a gentleman's wedding band to him, the one my grandfather had worn, because she had already donated it to the war crowd. "And besides," she told him, "it would have brought you only a world of ill luck, despair, and endless grief. When the war's over, I'll buy you a nice one. Do without until then." Mr. Baines thanked her, and then he went out to his car and brought in gifts for my grandmother, his mother, and me. He put them under the tree, asking me to make sure his mother opened hers and understood whom it was from.

Every time my grandmother said, "Sophia, you'd better call me," my mother promised to call from South Carolina.

When she was inside the car, my grandmother and I leaned in and held her. She snapped at my grandmother for knocking her hat off center and had me take the pins out and put it on straight again. When the hat was on right and the car door was shut, my grandmother was not by me. She had walked back to the house. She was standing on the top step, her hands somewhere over her stomach, lost in the folds and folds of dark brown crepe. I saw a hand emerge. It waved, then disappeared again.

That evening, my grandmother and I baked Christmas cookies. We decorated them using a hypodermic needle. It worked beautifully. Old Mrs. Baines ate the cookies faster than we could set them in front of her. We put her to bed in my mother's room and went to listen to Mr. Roosevelt's fireside chat. My grandmother stayed up for *Holiday with Strings,* but I dosed myself with some of my mother's evening primrose and went to bed, nursing, as I was, the great hole in my heart. I lay there and worried that my mother had just ruined another memory for herself, and I worried that she would return, pack her belongings, move out, and grow too lonesome. I had my grandmother, but all my mother would have while Mr. Baines worked was the old woman, the radio, volunteer work, books, and magazines. There would be a gap where my grandmother and I had been. Especially where my grandmother had been. She took up quite a bit of room in one's life. I worried what would happen when my mother started appearing at our door each morning, eager to stay there until it was time for Mr. Baines to come home from work. This was what I predicted for her. And I also foresaw big fights, when my grandmother would say things like, "Sophia! You finally have the life you wanted. Go live it!" I had to talk to my grandmother about this. I had to have her tell me how things would be, and so I went to her. She had turned all the lights off in the living room except for those on the

Christmas tree, and she was sitting there rocking, listening to Britten's *A Ceremony of Carols.* I told her all my worries. She said, "No. Sophia will be happy. So will you, and so will I. Go to sleep."

WHEN I AWAKENED early on
Christmas morning to slip my grandmother's presents underneath the tree, I saw that Santa Claus had come. My
grandmother had laid everything out, and now she sat in the
kitchen with Mrs. Baines. When my grandmother saw me,
she patted Mrs. Baines on the hand, moved her coffee over,
and put the cup between her palms. Then she got up,
walked over, and whispered into my ear, "I got her talking
about Lee. She remembers *seeing* him. Then I asked her
what I'd fed her for breakfast." My grandmother moved her
hands as if she were releasing doves into the air. She said,
"Gone. Gone entirely."

It occurred to me as we stood watching Mrs. Baines
talking to herself, fumbling around for memories, that we'd
not gotten her anything for Christmas. Mr. Baines had left
that large box for her, but I hated the thought of her
opening just that one thing while my grandmother and I

opened the ten or twelve boxes marked with our names. I told my grandmother, and she volunteered to let Mrs. Baines open all her gifts, so long as she didn't become attached to anything. So we called Mrs. Baines into the living room, exclaiming that Santa Claus had come.

I handed out presents, as this had always been my job. Then I sat down on the floor by the tree. There were several boxes left. I realized I had let my mother go without giving her my presents. They were all under the tree: *The G-String Murders* by Gypsy Rose Lee; a used though first edition of Edna Ferber's *So Big* to add to her collection; a beaded purse; two pairs of stockings I'd stood in line three hours to buy; and a renewal card for *True Story,* a gift my grandmother lamented each year even though, I knew, she read it on the sly. My grandmother had been more practical. She had paid for the reading glasses that had recently been prescribed for my mother. These tortoiseshell glasses were with her in South Carolina. My grandmother had also given her money to have her teeth, hair, and fingernails fixed, and a war bond that she said would finance my mother's shoe binges well into her dotage. I stacked all my mother's presents in a corner, for her to open on her return, and tried to think nothing else of her. But it was difficult. What was my mother doing at that moment? I asked my grandmother how she thought my mother was getting along, what she might be doing.

She said, "Same thing everybody's doing who got married last night."

I thought of my mother in bed with Mr. Baines, sleeping.

My mother, again, was having the time of her life. I left them there and joined the conversation my grandmother was trying to have with Mrs. Baines. It was about nothing more than the weather, but still, my grandmother had to take hold and drag the woman from subject to verb, as she strayed so wildly in between. Mrs. Baines was due to say which season she preferred, but instead she asked if she could open a present. I told her to go right ahead. She tore the paper off one of the boxes for my grandmother from Mr. Baines. My grandmother leaned way over into her, and when Mrs. Baines moved the tissue paper and uncovered the present, my grandmother shouted, "Good God! It's Lee!" I halfway expected the General to come riding up out of the box on his horse, that's how excited she was. She moved the box from Mrs. Baines's lap to her own and pulled out a volume of the Douglas Southall Freeman biography of Robert E. Lee. Although she could've held forth at great length on exactly where the General had gone wrong and why, she had wanted to read this biography. I asked whether she had mentioned it to Mr. Baines. She hadn't. He had read her mind. Mrs. Baines didn't complain about having the present removed from her lap. She was already tearing into the next one. It was another volume of the Lee biography. My grandmother was thrilled. She offered to help Mrs. Baines with the other boxes, sure as she was that she'd find the other two volumes. They were both there.

My grandmother started going through the books with a ferocious intensity, so I told Mrs. Baines to open the big box from her son. What was in there? A small oil painting of a white-columned brick house with ferns hanging the length of the porch. She held it up and propped it on her knees, turned so I could see it. She pointed to the painting the way librarians do when they're reading a picture book to a circle of children, and with a sudden clarity of mind she said, "This is my home. This is where I live." Then she turned it back around and smiled at it. I could see all those tossed and tumbled memories doing her the courtesy of sorting themselves out and lining up, marching out for her.

My grandmother had stopped riffling through her books. She looked at Mrs. Baines's face and then at the painting. I know she was seeing the same thing I was. Sitting there beside Mrs. Baines, she looked healthy and strong and safe in the knowledge that not one memory had ever left her. I doubted she would abide any slippage. She would demand to leave this world knowing everything she had ever known. As I sat by the Christmas tree, I realized how intimidating my grandmother would be to all those trillions of dead people who'd never met her.

Mr. Baines had been as kind to me as he had been to my grandmother. He gave me a crystal vanity box and a pearl bracelet. I opened all the presents I'd seen on the bed, and then my grandmother opened hers, or rather, Mrs. Baines opened them and my grandmother lifted them out of her lap. Nothing my mother and I gave her could compete with the Lee biography, but she was very gracious, making a fuss over each of the presents before she laid them to the side and started poring through the books again. My mother gave her a set of antique scalpels that had been used on Civil

War battlefields. She also gave her a pair of kid gloves and a recently reprinted leather-bound edition of Poe's *Tales of the Grotesque and Arabesque.* The latter was something my mother had most assuredly wanted for herself. She had achieved a reputation as an Indian giver. I gave my grandmother a pair of bookends, a copy of *The Years,* by Virginia Woolf, a writer for whom she had grieved the year before, and a framed snapshot Mr. Baines had taken of my mother and me a couple of weeks before. We were standing on our front steps, looking down at the camera. We had on matching Eisenhower jackets, and I was wearing the slacks my mother had bought and implored me to wear for the occasion. I hadn't wanted to. Nothing, at the time, could've been more unfamiliar to me. I felt as if I were dressing up in a Halloween costume. My mother assured me that I looked grand, thoroughly modern. That may have been the case, but I couldn't help tugging at the fabric between my thighs as I stood on those steps. Right before Mr. Baines snapped the picture, my mother reached over and moved my hand. "Margaret," she said, "that looks obscene. Stop it. Smile."

After lunch my grandmother said, "I'm bored. Let's take a ride in the car." We decided to drive out to the German POW camp that had just been established near Warrenton. Much had been made of the camp in the newspaper, and she was eager to see it. On the way there, she subtracted the year of Mrs. Baines's birth from hers, and she concluded that although Mrs. Baines was only seventeen years older, she belonged to another age. She said, "If you count Mrs. Baines's years with regard to what she has seen happen in

the world, she's much, much older than me." When I asked
for evidence of this, she said, "Appomattox, 1865. It was
another age, entirely." To me, it was not. I lumped everything that had happened from 1865 to 1929 into one pile.
At school, time had been organized this way. I told my
grandmother this, and she said, "No, it was another age."
For her to have divided time any other way would have
made rough contemporaries of Mrs. Baines and her. She
would have no part of this.

When we got about a mile from the camp, traffic slowed
to the point that I felt as though I were trapped driving in
the middle of a Christmas parade. Faces in the cars in front
of us and behind us were glued to the windows. Even my
grandmother was looking hard out of her window—one of
those highly infrequent reminders that she could be like
other people. Everybody knew the camp was empty, but
this didn't matter. We all just wanted to see where they
would be. It would take four months for soldiers from
Rommel's crew in North Africa to get there and immediately
astound the community by planting the grounds with
zinnias, verbena, and rows and rows of hibiscus. I'm sure
that for many spectators, it was merely something interesting
to do between opening presents and eating turkey dinners.

A large package was waiting for me when we got home
after dropping Mrs. Baines back with her nurse. It was from
Tom. I gathered it had been delivered by his father's all-
purpose courier. My grandmother, miraculously, left me
alone to open it. I read the card first. It said: "I couldn't
decide, so I gave you all my artifacts. I threw in the stockings

for good measure." Inside the package were a tiny ivory Buddha, an edition of Hawaiian love songs bound in hand-tooled leather, Chinese good-luck paper, a geisha fan, a program from the play *Pal Joey* signed by Gene Kelly, a ticket stub from the 1940 World Series, a snapshot of Tom's mother beaming down at President Roosevelt as he handed her a small plaque, two arrowheads, a Broughton High School detention slip from 1937 marked "Two hours for general attitude," a perfect report card of his, also from 1937, a pair of baby shoes, and a picture of him sitting in a goat cart, dated 1925. On the back of this picture was written: "Goat then ate Tom's new gloves." Underneath all this were two pairs of rayon stockings, which were scheduled for rationing and already in short supply. By the time I uncovered the stockings, I was crying so hard I could barely see them. I spread everything out on the kitchen table and called my grandmother into the room. When I asked what I could possibly give him in return, she told me to sit still until she returned. She brought me the easy-life charm the hanged man had given her. She said, "Meet him at the train station with it. Tell him how it was given to me by a revived man. Tell him it works, depending on your definition of easy."

THE TRAIN coming in from Asheville the next day was late, as most trains were those days. I stood on the platform and waited. I spotted his sister, and then I saw the rest of his family. My grandmother had told me as I left the house that they would be there, and she had encouraged me to introduce myself and assert my right to be there. So that's what I did. I walked over, held my hand out to his mother, and introduced myself. She was very gracious, saying, "Oh, how grand! Won't Tom be pleased?" Everybody else responded with variations of "Yes, indeed!" Her husband took my hand, shook it firmly, and told me he felt he already knew me. He looked like those *Punch* caricatures of Winston Churchill. He was completely round, and when he finished shaking my hand, he didn't return his hands to his pockets or to his sides. He placed them on either side of his stomach and drummed his fingers while he rocked back and forth on his heels. He had on very shiny shoes. Usually, wives tolerate husbands like this and hope they won't get out of hand in public, but Mrs. Hawkings squeezed his arm, smiled, and reminded him that my grandmother was the one she'd been talking about. She seemed to like him enormously. She was wearing slacks and a suede jacket, and I could tell she colored her hair, although the work was becoming and apparently expensive. The ease of her movements, her good looks and style reminded me of my mother. Her four daughters looked wholesome to the core, that sort of outdoorsy, vigorous appearance common to affluent young women who ride horses, shoot skeet, sail, things like that. They had on no makeup. None was called for. Tom's brother, whose slightly dissipated and world-weary expression I recognized from the society pages, seemed hung-over. His hand was weak and clammy. He acted as though he was afraid that if he extended himself too far, said or moved too much, he'd become ill. When his mother glared at him for not acting more thrilled to meet me, he moved away a few steps and lit a cigarette. If he had been wearing a sign around his neck, I could not have had an easier time recognizing the black sheep of this family. I was interested to see what happened when Tom arrived, how he fell into the group.

When he got off the train, he grabbed me and kissed me in front of them all. I remember I had so little idea of what to do that I sort of opened my mouth wide, like a fish, and let him take over. I wondered if our teeth were supposed to be clanging that way, and then I stumbled backward into his mother, causing her to fall into her husband. If he had been any less substantial, she would've fallen off the platform onto the tracks. The whole lot of them thought this hilarious, even the brother. Tom's father boomed out, "Do you like her, boy?" Tom said he certainly did. My mouth felt numb, as though he had smashed the nerve endings, chewing my lips off. I could smell lipstick, and that meant it was smeared up to my nostrils. My hat was hanging off the back of my head. I had never felt happier.

When I tried to excuse myself to go home, they would have no part of it. They told me I was going to their house for oyster stew. Tom's mother said, "And he's got Santa Claus to open! I'm sure the Nazi prisoners didn't give him any Santa Claus!" I told them I would go if I could call my grandmother when I got there. She'd be concerned about me. Tom's mother said she could come over also. Her husband would go pick her up. She insisted on it.

With all that settled, Tom drove my car to his house. At the first stoplight we came to, I gave him the charm and explained how my grandmother had come to have it. He said it was a swell gift. He took my hand, and even when he reached up to change gears he did not let it go.

My grandmother would not come. She was waiting for a call to get through to my mother. I asked her if she thought my mother should be told where I was. She said she intended to tell her everything. It was the right time. She sounded lonely, and I promised to be home before dark. During dinner I excused myself to call her back. I felt so guilty there in this loud, happy room, knowing my grandmother was by herself, waiting for the phone to ring. When

I called, the line was busy. I went back to the table and told them my grandmother must have been talking to my mother. I looked at Tom's sisters and said, "She's a newly-wed herself. She just married Richard Baines." Tom's father initiated a toast in her honor, and he insisted that I take a bottle of champagne home with me so my grandmother and I could do the same. The rest of the afternoon, I felt completely encircled by Tom's family.

My grandmother was eating dinner when I got home. I showed her the bottle of champagne and told her what it was for. She told me we'd have to wait until she felt better. She said, "I'd hate to help you drink something that expensive and then have it come up on me." I asked what was wrong, and she replied, "Nothing sleep won't cure. Half the patients I've had could track their problems to lack of sleep."

I asked whether she had spoken with my mother. She brightened. She said that she had and that my mother was fine. She and Mr. Baines were having a big time at the Atlantis. When I asked if she had told my mother about Tom, she brightened even more. She shouted, "You'd better sit down for this!"

I did, and then she squeezed my forearm and said, "She knew! She said she knew something was going on, and so she jimmied the lock on your cedar chest and read all the letters. So I said, 'Sophia! You've never kept anything to yourself. How'd you manage it?' She told me she didn't keep it to herself. She told Richard right away, and he told her that if you had wanted her to know, you would've told her. He convinced her to leave you alone. He told her you'd appreciate it. How about that? You've played cards with her a thousand times. You know how her face shows everything she's got in her hand. But she did it."

I felt as ill as Tom's brother looked, thinking of my mother going after the lock on my cedar chest with a nail file, reading everything, putting it all back in as carefully as I'd packed those Red Cross boxes. My grandmother could see this playing through my mind. She said, "Don't worry. It's nothing your mother hasn't been exposed to. All those cheap novels. All those *True Story* articles. Think of it!"

I said, "But *True Story* has never done an article about me! Tom wrote some pretty personal things in those last letters."

She said, "That's what Sophia told me. She said you could just see him up there, tickled over having bribed his way into the Fitzgerald room, quoting Jay Gatsby to you. But don't worry about it. Your mother's fine. She's not going to tease you, if that's what you're worried about. She's glad he's decent, smart, rich, and everything else. And anyway, Richard and she will come home joined at the waist, like Siamese twins. She'll not be into your affairs. You go on about your business."

I asked when she was supposed to call my mother again, and she told me it would be the following morning. She had asked my mother not to phone us because of the added expense of a collect call. It was taking the phone company eight to ten hours to place long-distance calls, and so my grandmother was putting in the order before she went to bed. I had hoped it wasn't for a couple of days. I needed time to gather my wits. It would be the first conversation I'd had with my mother in which I was an equal. We would talk about something besides war news, books, movies, my grandmother, college, my mother's disappointing marriage to my father, her disappointment that my appeal to young men appeared stunted, dwarflike compared with what hers had been. I wondered whether at that moment my mother was lying in her honeymoon bed with her new husband, staring at him, as in awe of her new life as I was of mine.

MY GRANDMOTHER beat me to the phone. By the time I got there, she had the receiver cradled on her neck and was trying to pull a tall stool over with her foot. I pulled it the rest of the way, and she sat down, ignoring me. "Sophia!" she shouted. "This is your mother! Can you hear me?"

My grandmother had led the way with the indoor toilet, but long-distance calling was another matter. She always shouted until the person on the other end assured her that she could be heard. When my mother told her she could hear her, my grandmother started speaking normally. She said, "Good, and yes, Margaret seems to have had a fine time. What?"

She listened and then told me to run outside and bring the morning paper in to her. I did. She turned to Eleanor Roosevelt's "My Day" column and told my mother to talk to me while she read it through.

I took the phone. My mother asked me right off if I'd liked Tom's family. I said I had. Then she asked what my plans were for the rest of the holidays. I steadied myself and told her she already knew what they were. She was quiet, and then she apologized. She sounded so thoroughly earnest, and while I was considering how to respond to her, she said, "Well? So are you going to use the discounts or not? I know what I'd do." I told her I was embarrassed by what she had done, and she asked me if I was going to chastise her repeatedly. She said, "I did it, and I'm sorry. I truly am. What else do you want me to say?" I told her I didn't know, but yes, I was thinking about using the discounts. I'd stayed up late the night before, thinking about all I wanted, starting with a formal gown. I wanted something sequined, the sort of dress that attracts a great deal of dangerous attention. I wanted matching shoes, and while I was at it, I wanted a handbag, a permanent wave, a manicure, makeup, and a facial. She screamed, "What? Is this Margaret?" I told her she had heard me right, and when I handed the receiver to my grandmother she had to wipe it on her robe. My palms had sweated all over it. I was trembling as well.

She listened to my mother a moment, looked at me hard, and said, "I wouldn't say Margaret's *changed,* but let me wait and give you my verdict after she comes home from the beauty shop." She winked at me and then told my mother she had been correct in saying that Mrs. Roosevelt's column was the most ridiculous one yet. I read the column while she offered my mother a scathing and hilarious commentary. Mrs. Roosevelt said she intended to go right out shopping and catch all the after-Christmas sales. She planned to buy ahead for next year. My grandmother told my mother, "Now Eleanor's children know to expect something shopworn, broken, or otherwise mauled next year." The Roosevelts, she said, were made of money, rolling in it, stinking with it. Together, she and my mother created a picture of Eleanor Roosevelt in some department store in Washington, rummaging through the sale racks, hunting down the best bargains. I put my ear close to the receiver. My mother was laughing uproariously, adding more details about Eleanor's hounding clerks for even deeper markdowns, pointing out dropped stitches in sweaters, inquiring after the colorfastness of a blouse, threatening to make the store pay for ruined laundry if the color ran, being pushy all around.

My grandmother held the phone out to me again. I was afraid my mother would question me about my sudden desire to fix myself up, but she didn't. She offered me her velvet dress and her double strand of pearls. If that didn't suit me, I could get anything I wanted and consider it a late Christmas gift. I thanked her, and I thanked her also for all the things she had already given me, especially the earrings. She said she was looking forward to coming home and opening her own Santa Claus. We were to keep the tree up for her. "When I get back, we'll have another Christmas morning," she said. "You know we'll have a good time, because we always do."

A popular cosmetics advertisement of the day said, "Give looking pretty your all." I spent the four hours before Tom's sister's piano recital doing just that. I'd never spent so much time on myself, and I recall wondering how women who did this regularly had adequate strength left to enjoy themselves. I did everything I had seen my mother do, starting at the top of my head and working down. My grandmother predicted that Tom would whistle through his teeth and say I looked swell. She had taken a bath, dusted herself with her Mavis powder, brushed her hair, and put on her mother's Sherman dress and those ancient shoes. When she caught my eyes fixed on her shoes, she said, "They're polished. If the boy's family takes issue with my shoes, I can always remove them." My closet looked so bleak that I went into my mother's. I tried on everything she had. I chose a black georgette skirt and a white organza surplice blouse tied by a side bow. If I could've gotten into her velvet dress, I would've. Two years' worth of sitting around reading had given me what she called "office hips," and when I had to call my grandmother in to zip me, and then listen to her memories of cramming her sisters into corsets, I pledged myself to a slenderizing program. She told me I should get on this right away, unless I wanted to spend my honeymoon undressing in the dark.

When Tom arrived to pick me up, he did not whistle through his teeth but he did say I looked swell. My grandmother could have told him how long it took me to accomplish this, but she didn't. She told him to come with her. She wanted to show him some things. She led him all around the house, commenting on her collection of antique surgical implements and the homemade nativity scene she had accepted in lieu of payment for delivering a set of twins. He liked this particularly, the way the Wise Men's calico headpieces were held on by Nehi bottle caps, the way Mary tipped over if she wasn't wedged up next to Joseph. He said it reminded him of the strange crucifix he'd seen in the hospital. I tried to tell him I knew which one he meant. I wanted to tell him what I had imagined about it, but my grandmother led him away before I could. She took him into the long hall and showed him how lovely my mother had been upon her graduation from Miss Nash's School, how feisty she looked in the picture Mr. Baines took of her at Grandfather Mountain. She pointed to one taken of me in the first grade and said, "Margaret read *The Jungle Book* that year." Then she pointed to my second-grade picture and said, "She read *Kidnapped* that year. It scared her teacher to death. This same thing had happened when her mother slipped my copy of *The Mysterious Stranger* off to school with her. That was in 1917. Her teacher thought Twain was a nut. He was not a nut. He got some strange ideas there toward the end, but he was not dangerous, as Miss Nash led those girls to believe. I tried to make the woman show me the evil in Twain's story about the frog contest, and she could not. She would've had them read Sir Walter Scott continuously if she'd had her way. Sir Walter Scott. I almost pulled Sophia out of the school over the reading list, except they seemed to be making such headway teaching her enough manners to operate in good company."

She would have rambled on in this very uncharacteristic fashion had Tom not waited for her to take a breath and said we should leave for the recital. His mother was hoping we could get there a little early. Without a word, my grandmother walked down the hall. When she got to the end, she turned around to me and said, "So very much has happened. Am I correct?" I told her she was, and then I collected her coat and gloves for her. She rode quietly all the way to town.

MY MEMORY has allowed me to keep that afternoon perfectly intact. I can see the inside of Tom's mother's car. It was a mess. He had to move piles of paper over so my grandmother could sit down. He said his mother read mail while sitting in the post office parking lot and threw it over her shoulder into the backseat, and there it remained until his father needed to pay bills. He'd scrounge around, find what he needed, and leave the rest.

As we drove away from our house, I saw Nathaniel's mother in her yard, lifting the top off a trashcan. She was wearing an olive corduroy jacket with two large pockets in front. She looked up at us and wondered why my grandmother and I were riding off with a stranger. Halfway to town I saw one boy pulling another in a wagon. The boy riding in the wagon was wearing a black woolen hat pulled down almost over his eyes. He had on a plaid shirt that looked too thin for late December. I remember thinking,

But he's got the hat. My grandmother had lectured people for years about how much heat escapes through a bare head.

When we got to the auditorium, it appeared that the whole town had turned out for the performance. A crowd was outside, moving in slowly. Tom said his mother had called in all her markers. "Every lawmaker she has not maligned lately is here. She's likely to take attendance so she can really give the absentees the business. She didn't want my sister embarrassed." There she was at the door, waiting for us, or rather, for my grandmother. She apologized that her husband wasn't there to greet us. He was backstage with their other children. All the way to our reserved seats, she told my grandmother what a joy it was to meet her. She said she would've called or written her years before, had she not been so intimidated.

My grandmother thanked her, took her seat, and then more or less held court for the few minutes until the program started. Tom's mother sat on the edge of her seat, ready to introduce my grandmother to the people coming forward to greet her. No introductions were needed. The judge who had committed the boy against her advice was there, and he came up to her. The dean of the medical school at Chapel Hill who through the years had sent her articles told her he had one sitting on his desk, waiting to be sent out to her the next week, about all the new antibiotic therapy. The pharmacist from Hayes Barton was there. He told her she looked grand, to which she responded, "Thank you, but my blood is running poorly, my head hurts, and my stomach is churning. I know I look rotten as Satan." He told

248

her to come by the pharmacy and fill her pockets up with iron tablets. The new head of the Rural Midwifery Council came forward and told my grandmother of everyone's complaints that she wasn't doing everything as swiftly, creatively, and effectively as my grandmother had during her years in charge. My grandmother told her she was sorry, and then recommended the woman interview some of the old granny midwives in the county if she wanted a better view of her job. "But don't worry yourself too much over it," she said. "Everything's petering out. All these girls, colored and white, want to go to the hospital and deliver, as well they should." While she was saying this, I could hear Tom's sister behind the curtain, practicing her scales at lightning speed.

She opened with Chopin's "Revolutionary Étude," then played Grieg's E Minor Piano Sonata and Bach's Minuet in G. After these Tom whispered to me that his sister had wanted to play the more complicated and sophisticated pieces she'd mastered at Juilliard, but his mother had reminded her that this wasn't New York. She went on to *Woodland Sketches* and then closed with Ravel's *Le Tombeau de Couperin.* I remember how still the audience was during this last piece. It had been written in honor of Ravel's friends who had died in the Great War.

Tom, my grandmother, and I arrived at his house for the reception before any of the other guests. He took my grandmother's coat and said, "Now I'm going to show you *my*

house." He led her around, as she had led him earlier that day. She seemed very pliant, letting him hold her hand and take her from here to there. He showed her the pictures of his mother standing next to everyone from William Randolph Hearst to William Allen White. He said she met everybody who blew through town. He showed her a picture of himself receiving his Eagle Scout badge. He took her to the grand piano and told her that it had been his grandmother's and that Sarah Bernhardt had offered her top dollar for it, as she thought the tone did justice to her voice. Miss Bernhardt had spent a weekend with his grandmother when she was in Raleigh for a performance. His grandmother was remarkable in many ways. Among other things, she had taught Clara Bow how to make buttermilk biscuits and Gertrude Ederle how to fly-fish.

He was showing my grandmother his sisters' thimble collection when people started arriving, and he excused himself to go to the door. She seemed fascinated with the thimbles; she took one and held it up to the light, put it back, and took another. "Margaret," she said, "this is *some* family." I agreed that it was, and then told her we'd leave whenever she felt tired. I said, "Unless the business about poor blood was a ruse to get free iron tablets." She told me she'd let me know when she needed to leave.

We stayed for an hour. In that time she managed to astound everyone present by taking a bothersome wart off the right hand of Tom's pianist sister. My grandmother noticed it and asked, with not a great deal of tact, how she played the piano with that thing. Tom's sister said it worried her considerably, but she was afraid of having it cut off. My grandmother said, "I'll do it. I'll do it and you'll be rid of it." Tom's sister asked if it would hurt, and my grandmother told her it would, but only for a few minutes. The guests were choosing sides in a discussion of whether or not she would accept my grandmother's impromptu offer to take this wart off right here, right now. Tom's mother said, "Oh, go ahead!" Her daughter thought it over a bit more and then told my grandmother she was welcome to set up her operating theater in her bedroom. I asked my grandmother what I could do and was told to gather all the usual supplies from the kitchen and medicine cabinet and bring them in to her.

Tom showed me where everything was. He kept saying I had no idea what this meant to his mother. She'd talk about it for years. When he let me into his sister's bedroom, she was sitting on one side of a table with her hand poised in the air as if waiting for my grandmother to manicure her. I had put a paring knife, two hand towels, and a bottle of Merthiolate on one of those Coca-Cola trays with the Gibson girl on them. My grandmother thanked me and said she'd be out in a minute.

I went back to the party with Tom, wondering whether the Victrola would drown out what I knew lay ahead. However, there were no screams. My grandmother came in and pronounced the patient very brave. She said she had left her in her room, applying pressure to the wound. She'd be out soon. Then my grandmother excused herself. I knew she was going to the bathroom to clean the paring knife and the tray before they were returned to the kitchen. I followed her, offering to help. She said, "Better than that. I'll let you do it. I'm feeling whipped." She sat on a slipper chair in the bathroom while I washed the things, and when I was done, she stood and said, "Think of the living I could make removing warts door to door. Maybe that could be my new line." I didn't know how to respond. Where my grandmother was concerned, there was no precedent for self-deprecation.

When we got home, my grandmother drank gingerroot tea to relieve what she termed an "irritatingly vague nausea," and then took papaya tablets for her indigestion. I told her she should lie down. She refused, saying that would make things worse. She intended to keep moving, and thus drive the pain out of her system. She'd move about all night if she had to. I left her in the living room, standing in the middle of the floor, lifting one leg and then the other, touching her hands to her shoulders. Both actions were done to the tick of the Pasquotank mantel clock. That's how I went to sleep, hearing those high-top shoes clomp, clomp, clomp.

Usually I would hear her in the morning. I would hear her taking the marble mortar and pestle out of the cabinet, and then I would hear her get out a cutting board and a broad knife. This is when I would get up and go to her. My mother would be leaning against the counter drinking coffee or sitting at the table working the crossword puzzle. I cannot recall a time that my mother didn't say, "Margaret, you've got two choices. Raw garlic on toast, or cereal." I always chose the cereal. That morning, I didn't hear anything. I got up and saw my grandmother hadn't slept in her bed, so I went to look for her. I found her sitting in the mohair chair, slumped to the side. She had sat down, tired, I imagined, of marching in place, and had died sometime during the night.

I dialed the operator and pleaded with her to put my call through. She was sympathetic, but she couldn't do anything. I would have to wait for a line to my mother. I screamed that I couldn't wait, and then I hung up. I phoned Dr. Nutter at his home. He told me he could place the call. He would talk to my mother, and then he would drive to my house. He said I should have a neighbor or a friend to come stay with me until he got there. I was so grateful to be told what to do. I called Tom and told him what had happened. He said he'd come right away. I thanked him, and after I hung up I stood by the phone, wondering what I was supposed to do with myself.

Then I knew. I went to the linen closet and took out as many towels as I could carry. I brought them into the living room and dropped them in the middle of the floor. Then I went back, got an armload of sheets, and dropped them on top of the towels. We had so many mirrors—I had no idea how many until I started draping them. Then I moved to the pictures, turning them to the wall or placing them facedown on the furniture. I stopped the clock in my room first, then moved to the others in the house. I had to stand on the tall stool to reach the one on the kitchen wall. All that was left was the mantel clock from Pasquotank County. I opened the little glass door and stopped the hands. Everything seemed to have been done. I sat on the sofa and watched my grandmother there across the room. I hadn't done everything. The miniature railroad watch pinned to her bosom had to be stopped. I had to get up, go over to her, and touch her to stop it. I stared at her, for how long I cannot say. And then I stood up and walked over to her and pulled the tiny gold pin up with my fingernails.

Now everything was done, and I told her so. I sat down on the floor by her and said, "There. See how I knew what to do?" I looked at her mouth, slightly open. Her lips were dry. She hadn't purged. She had always said all she needed to say, and so there were no secret longings, no secret wishes and desires that had never been spoken. I was glad for that. I smoothed my great-grandmother's dress across my grandmother's knees and ran my hand across the toes of their resolute shoes. And then I lay down, rested my head by her feet, and waited to be found.